P9-BZO-971

3 1265 01541 1622

OFFICIALLY
WITHDRAWN

Nov 2016

★ *the* ★

KINDNESS
CLUB

Chloe on the Bright Side

the ★ ★
KINDNESS
CLUB
Chloe on the Bright Side

COURTNEY SHEINMEL

BLOOMSBURY
NEW YORK   LONDON   OXFORD   NEW DELHI   SYDNEY

PALATINE PUBLIC LIBRARY DISTRICT
700 N. NORTH COURT
PALATINE, ILLINOIS 60067-8159

Copyright © 2016 by Courtney Sheinmel
All rights reserved. No part of this book may be reproduced or transmitted in any form
or by any means, electronic or mechanical, including photocopying, recording, or by any
information storage and retrieval system, without permission in writing from the publisher.

First published in the United States of America in November 2016
by Bloomsbury Children's Books
www.bloomsbury.com

Bloomsbury is a registered trademark of Bloomsbury Publishing Plc

For information about permission to reproduce selections from this book, write to
Permissions, Bloomsbury Children's Books, 1385 Broadway, New York, New York 10018
Bloomsbury books may be purchased for business or promotional use. For information
on bulk purchases please contact Macmillan Corporate and Premium Sales Department at
specialmarkets@macmillan.com

Library of Congress Cataloging-in-Publication Data
Names: Sheinmel, Courtney.
Title: Chloe on the bright side / Courtney Sheinmel.
Description: New York : Bloomsbury, [2016] | Series: The Kindness Club
Summary: Rejected by the cool girls' club, fifth-grader Chloe Silver, new in town after
her parents' divorce, forms a different type of club, with offbeat Lucy Tanaka and
nerdy Theo Barnes, that tests out different acts of kindness on classmates.
Identifiers: LCCN 2015049960 (print) | LCCN 2016011737 (e-book)
ISBN 978-1-68119-091-4 (hardcover) • ISBN 978-1-68119-092-1 (e-book)
Subjects: | CYAC: Clubs—Fiction. | Friendship—Fiction. | Kindness—Fiction. |
Schools—Fiction. | Moving, Household—Fiction. | Divorce—Fiction. |
BISAC: JUVENILE FICTION / Social Issues / Friendship. | JUVENILE FICTION /
School & Education.
Classification: LCC PZ7.S54124 Ch 2016 (print) | LCC PZ7.S54124 (e-book) | DDC [Fic]—dc23
LC record available at http://lccn.loc.gov/2015049960

Book design by Colleen Andrews
Typeset by NewGen Knowledge Works (P) Ltd., Chennai, India
Printed and bound in the U.S.A. by Berryville Graphics Inc., Berryville, Virginia
2 4 6 8 10 9 7 5 3 1

All papers used by Bloomsbury Publishing, Inc., are natural, recyclable products
made from wood grown in well-managed forests. The manufacturing processes
conform to the environmental regulations of the country of origin.

For Chloe & Anabelle Swidler

Be kind to one another.
—*Ellen DeGeneres*

CLUB

Chloe on the Bright Side

I have the best friends in my new school.

I'd been repeating that sentence in my head for a couple of weeks, ever since Mom had brought me along to see Regan Halliday, her old college roommate and soon-to-be new boss. Regan was the reason Mom had picked the town of Braywood, Maryland, for us to move to over the summer. I'd be starting fifth grade at the Braywood Intermediate School and Mom would be Regan's new office manager. It was a perfect opportunity for us to have a fresh start, Mom said.

Mom had been Dad's office manager at his dental practice since before I was born. But when my parents decided to split up, working together wasn't an option anymore. The week before school started, Mom said we should drop by

Regan's office to say hi. I hadn't realized that "saying hi" would include Mom leaving me in the waiting room while she went in the back to talk business. To be fair, I don't think Mom did either, or she probably would've told me to bring my summer reading along. Incidentally, summer reading was something I hadn't had at my old school, but when we got my registration forms, there was a book list included. I picked *The League of Unexceptional Children.*

But I didn't have the book with me that day. Instead, I grabbed a magazine from the pile on the waiting room coffee table. The actress Erin Lindstrom was on the cover. In the article about her, she said the secret to her success was something called "affirmations." Basically, if she wanted something to happen, she would say a sentence in her head like it already had. Doing that activated her subconscious mind and helped her achieve her goals. It was how she landed the starring role in *Letters Never Sent,* which got her an Academy Award.

So there was the bright side of accompanying Mom on her errand: I learned about affirmations.

I have the best friends in my new school.

It had been in my head every day since, but especially on the morning of Book Pickup Day, which was another different thing about Braywood Intermediate. On the Friday before classes began, you had to go to school to pick up all the syllabi and textbooks you'd need for the year.

I'd practiced the walk to my new school a couple times with Mom, but I did it by myself for the first time on Book Pickup Day. Mom said she'd bring the car to get me after, since I'd have a lot to carry on the way home. Plus she wanted to take me to the Standing Oaks Mall to get a new fall jacket. I'd grown out of my old one.

I got to school and followed the signs from the parking lot to the gymnasium. My affirmation was running around my brain in a loop, like a song on repeat:

I have the best friends in my new school. I have the best friends in my new school. I have the best friends in my new school.

Inside the gym, rows of tables had been set up, with piles of books on each of them. I didn't know where to start, and I wished that my best friend Lia Marin was a new girl along with me. She was better at approaching people and asking about whatever it was she needed to know the answer to.

I stood there for a couple minutes, looking around at the tables of books, and at the kids, too. There were at least a couple hundred of them. It was weird not knowing any of their names, and not knowing who would be my friend. At that moment it felt like when I went to the pet store with

Dad, and we stood in front of a cage of bunnies deciding which one to take home with us. Actually, now it felt more like *I* was the bunny hoping to get picked. I felt a sudden pang for Captain Carrot. I hoped someone would pick me, the way I'd picked him.

So far, no one was picking me. Across the room, I spotted a big sign that said REGISTRATION, and three tables under it, with smaller signs that said A–F, G–R, and S–Z.

I headed over to the third table and gave my name to the woman sitting behind it. She flipped through a bunch of papers and found the one marked "SILVER, CHLOE" on top. "Here's your schedule. I'll be seeing you for fourth-period Spanish." She tapped her name, Señora Rivera. "Go on and get your books."

"Thanks," I told her.

"Oh, wait," she said. "You forgot a pencil case. Everyone gets a pencil case." She handed me a yellow one, with "Braywood Intermediate School" printed in black letters on the side.

"*Muchas gracias,*" I said, which is the Spanish way to say "thank you very much."

"*De nada,*" she told me with a smile. "*Hasta el lunes.*"

I stepped away to let the girl behind me get her schedule. "Hi, I'm Lucy Tanaka," she told Señora Rivera, while I read over the list of books I'd need for each class. I was about to head over to the other side of the room to get them, when

I heard Lucy Tanaka say, "Can I get a yellow case instead of green?"

"Sorry, I just gave away my last yellow. How about blue or red?"

"No, thanks," she said. "I guess green will be okay."

I turned toward her. Lucy Tanaka had slick black hair and was wearing a dress that looked a bit like a man's shirt. There was a belt around her waist that reminded me of one of the tassels that Mom had bought to tie back the curtains in our new living room. "Do you want to trade?" I asked.

"Really?"

"Sure. I don't mind a green one."

"Wow, thanks." She handed it over, and I gave her the yellow one. "The green case matches your eyes," she told me. "You look good holding it. I swear I'm not just saying that because I want you to trade."

"I know you're not," I told her. "We already traded, after all."

"Exactly," Lucy Tanaka said. "What's your name?"

"Chloe Silver," I said.

"Nice to meet you," she said. "And thanks again."

"You're welcome."

After that, I headed to the book tables. In front of me a girl in a silver T-shirt and white jeans was loading up her arms with about a dozen books. She reminded me of Trissa Thompson from my old school. Trissa had light brown skin and she usually wore her hair twisted up in a tight bun. This girl was pale-skinned. Her wavy brown hair was loose and came down just past her shoulders. But she looked confident, like she knew people would want to be her friend. That's how Trissa was.

Lia and I had *sort of* been friends with Trissa, though not as close as we'd wanted to be. I knew if Lia were with me, she'd want to be close friends with this girl. She'd probably start talking to her. I stood there, thinking of my affirmation, hoping it would make the right words come out of my mouth.

And then *the girl* started talking to *me!*

Well, not to me, exactly. But close enough to give me a chance to talk back to her. What she said, to no one in particular, was, "Ugh. Figures I'd get the worst itch on my back when I don't have any free arms to scratch it."

So then I said, "I could scratch it for you, if you want."

She turned around. "I have a free hand," I added. "It'd be easy for me to do."

The girl's eyes moved up and down quickly, sizing me up. "Actually, that would be great," she said. "It's on the left side. By my shoulder." I scratched. "A little higher," she said. "A little lower. Ooh, that's just right." Then she laughed to herself. "I sound like Goldilocks. Thanks. That's much better."

"Hey, Monroe," another girl called, racing over.

"Rachael, OMG," the girl with the formerly itchy back said. "Did you see—"

Before she could finish her sentence, the textbook on the top of the pile in her arms slipped to the floor. The other girl—Rachael—and I both reached down to grab it. I got it first: *Beginner's Spanish*.

"That textbook's on my list, too," I said, standing back up.

"You must be in fifth grade then," Rachael said.

I nodded and slipped the Spanish book back on top of the pile in Monroe's arms. She had a silver cuff bracelet on her right forearm. "Your bracelet is really cool," I told her. "I saw a picture of Erin Lindstrom wearing one just like it."

"I'll tell my mom to tell her."

"Tell *Erin Lindstrom*?" I asked, incredulous. "Your mom *knows* her?"

"Yeah."

"Wow. Have you ever met her?"

"Once or twice," Monroe said, in a voice like it was no big thing, which was another difference. If someone from my old school had a mom who knew someone as famous as Erin Lindstrom, it would be a VERY big thing. "So, did you just move here?"

"Over the summer."

"Well, you should know Look Now at the Standing Oaks Mall is the best place to shop. That's where I got this." She gestured toward the bracelet with her chin.

"My mom and I are going to the mall right after this," I said. "I'll definitely look for it."

"Wait a sec," Rachael said. "You can't get the same thing as Monroe."

"Relax, Rach," Monroe said. "It's a free country. Besides, Erin Lindstrom has it, too." She turned to me. "Thanks for the Spanish book—and the back scratch."

"You're welcome."

"What were you saying before?" Rachael asked her.

"Oh," Monroe said. "I was about to ask if you saw what *she* was wearing today."

"I did," Rachael said. "To be honest I thought it wasn't that bad. Remember when she wore that vest of patches?"

"How could I forget? She had a new patch every day. Ms. Smit finally made her take it off when she added the one with the bells on it."

The two of them laughed. I wondered who they were talking about. But mostly I wondered whether Monroe would say something to me again. They were standing right by me, but we weren't exactly standing together. If I walked away, she probably wouldn't notice. Rachael, either. This was the hardest part about being the new kid—everyone else already had their friends all set. They didn't need me.

But Erin Lindstrom was right about one thing—my affirmation kept me focused on my goal.

"Hello, hello, hello!" a voice boomed. A tallish, baldish man came over and gave Rachael a fist bump. He couldn't fist-bump Monroe because of the books in her arms, so he bumped her elbow gently with his. Then he looked over at me. "I don't believe we've met before."

"I just moved here," I explained.

"Welcome," he said. He held out a fist, and I bumped it with mine. "I'm the principal, Mr. Dibble."

"I'm Chloe," I told him. "Chloe Silver."

"It's a pleasure to meet you," he said. "What grade are you in?"

"I'm starting fifth."

"Same with these two," Mr. Dibble said. "I assume they're showing you the Braywood Welcome Wagon spirit."

I nodded, shyly.

"Excellent," he said. "What teachers do you all have?"

"Danos," Monroe said.

"*Ms.* Danos," Mr. Dibble said. "She's wonderful."

"I have Mr. Goldfarb," Rachael said, giving Monroe a sad face.

"Mr. Goldfarb is also wonderful," Mr. Dibble said. "You should know, Ms. Silver, that we have nothing but wonderful teachers here at our school."

"I'm also in Ms. Danos's class," I told him.

"Well, Ms. Reeser," he said, turning to Monroe. "Can I count on you to show your new classmate the ropes on Monday?"

"Sure," she said.

"Excellent," he said again. "Why don't you stop by my office at lunchtime and let me know how your first day is going. Okay?"

"Okay," I said.

"Mr. Dibble!" someone called from across the room.

"I'm sorry, girls. It seems I'm being paged," he told us. "But I think we have everything squared away here, right?"

"You bet," Monroe told him.

He crossed the room in a few long strides, bumping fists and elbows along the way. Rachael said good-bye to me.

"'Bye," Monroe said. Then she added, "Hey, you know what? You should wear a french braid on Monday."

Rachael spun around. "Really?" she asked.

"Yes," Monroe said, nodding firmly. She turned back to me. "Not a regular braid. A french braid. On Monday."

"Okay," I said.

They said good-bye for real and walked off. I went to pick up my own school books. I barely noticed the weight of them as I walked out to Mom's car. I was too busy thinking about the bright side to Book Pickup Day. I hadn't wanted my parents to split up, and I hadn't wanted to move. But maybe some things would work out after all.

CHAPTER 2

After we finished up at the mall, Mom took me over to Dad's.

I spent every other weekend at Dad's new condo, plus Wednesday nights. It was kind of a pain to be passed back and forth like a baton in a relay race. But on the bright side, Mom and Dad each said I could paint my new room any color that I liked. I couldn't decide between Peppermint Tea (light green) or Fancy Pancy (lavender). But another bright side was that I didn't have to decide. After all, there were two bedrooms to paint.

Late Saturday afternoon, I was sitting at my desk in my peppermint room at Dad's condo. I had finished my book, and I had no idea what to do next. At my old school we had to write short book reports on index cards. I decided to do that, just in case, which was what I was doing when Dad knocked on my door. "Come in," I said.

"Hey, Chloe-Bear, I'm back," he said. Chloe-Bear is the nickname that Dad has had for me since forever. I roll my eyes whenever he uses it. But secretly, I kind of like it.

I rolled my eyes at him. "Did you get everything?" I asked. Dad had gone out to the supermarket to get the dough and fixings for our usual Saturday Make-Your-Own-Pizza Night.

"Of course I did," he told me.

"Good job, Jimbo," I said. Jimbo is my nickname for Dad. I also sometimes call him Daddy-o, or Big Jim.

He stepped all the way into the room and came over to my desk. "How's the report coming?"

"Pretty good, I think."

"That's my girl." He put his hands on my shoulders and gave them a squeeze.

"I'm a little bit worried about Monday, though," I admitted. I couldn't talk about it with Mom because I didn't want to upset her. She was sad enough on her own already. But telling Dad seemed safe. "I've never been the new kid in school before—well, except for when I was five years old and everyone was new, which doesn't count. Plus I had Lia."

Lia and I had always lived across the street from each other, but we didn't become best friends until a sandwich incident on our first day in kindergarten. We were a good pair because we complemented each other so well. She was bold when I was shy, so we got invited to more things. And I remembered things that she forgot, so when she left her spelling list behind at school on the night before a test, all she had to do was run across the street to borrow mine. We had all kinds of traditions, the way best friends do. Like whenever our favorite singer had a new song coming out, we'd listen to it on "Repeat" until we both had the whole thing memorized. We made up choreographed dances, too. And on Sunday evenings either her parents or mine would take us to Magic Cone, the ice-cream place in town. I would order Fudge Ripple Swirl, and Lia would order Cookie Dough Chip. When we'd each eaten half of our cones, one of us would yell "Switch!" and we'd trade.

"Making new friends is going to be easy for you," Dad told me now. "When you meet Sage tonight you'll see how easy it is."

Dad had been telling me about Sage Tofsky for the past few weeks. He'd met her and her mom, Gloria, in the laundry room of their building, and they'd struck up a conversation. Sage was ten, same as me, and of course Dad decided she'd be my new friend in the building. He said he would've introduced us earlier, but Sage had been on a camping trip with her dad the last time I was visiting. Apparently her parents were divorced, too.

"It'll be like having Lia across the street again," Dad said.

"I can't just replace Lia like that," I told him. "She's irreplaceable!"

Dad sighed and squeezed my shoulders again. "I know she is, bear. But on Monday you'll start making new friends by your mom's house."

"I might have done that already," I said, thinking of Monroe and Rachael.

"You see," Dad said. "I want you to have friends here, too." There was a bit of sadness in his voice, and in a weird way that made me feel kind of happy. After all, he was the one who decided to split up our family. Well, I guess Mom was also in on the decision, because she agreed to it. But the point is no one asked me what I thought about it.

For the record, if they'd asked me, I would've said: no way!

"You'll like Sage, I promise," Dad said, with that same sad voice, and I started to feel guilty—even though it wasn't my fault. Feelings can be so complicated sometimes.

"I'll finish this card and then I'll help you start cooking," I told him.

"No rush," Dad said. "We aren't going to the Tofskys for"—he twisted his wrist to check his watch—"another hour or so."

"We're going *to* the Tofskys?"

"You knew that," Dad said.

"I didn't."

"You did."

"Then why'd you buy the groceries?"

"To bring to them," Dad said. "I could've sworn I told you."

I shook my head. "We always cook dinner on Saturday nights. It's tradition."

"We'll still do the cooking," Dad said. "Just in another kitchen—with a couple extra sous chefs. Okay?"

"Yeah. Okay. So we'll make pizza at the Tofskys."

"I thought we'd shake things up a bit and do something else instead," Dad said.

"What? But we always do pizza on Saturday nights. That's also tradition."

"Sage has celiac disease," Dad said.

"She has a disease?" I asked, and I felt something twist deep in my stomach. Poor Sage.

"Don't worry, it's manageable," Dad said. "It means she's gluten intolerant and she can't eat certain things."

"Oh."

"Besides, we've only done three Saturday pizza dinners. I'd hardly call that a tradition."

I was with Dad every other weekend, so three Saturdays added up to six weeks of tradition. But given Sage's situation, I didn't press the point. "What are we making instead?" I asked.

"Caesar salad and lemon chicken," he said.

"And your famous chocolate chip cookies for dessert?" I asked hopefully.

"No can do," Dad said. "Flour has gluten in it. But I bought fruit and ice cream to bring with us. Fudge Ripple Swirl."

"I love that flavor," I said.

"I know."

"Thanks, Dad," I said. "Hey, you know, if you don't mind going out again, we should probably get some flowers for Gloria and Sage. People love getting flowers."

"That's a great idea," Dad said.

I pushed back my chair. "Let's go right now."

"Did you finish your book report?" Dad asked.

"I'm not even sure I need to do one."

"How about this—you work on your report, just in case. I'll run out and get the flowers. Roses, maybe. Pink ones?"

"Yellow ones," I said. "They mean friendship."

"Why is that?" Dad asked.

"I'm not sure," I told him. "I just know that they do."

"All right then," he said. "Yellow flowers it is. I'm proud of you, Chloe-Bear. You are such a thoughtful kid." He kissed the top of my head. "I'll see you soon."

CHAPTER 3

I finished my index card and called Lia to fill her in on Book Pickup Day. By the time we hung up, Dad was back and it was time to go to the Tofskys. They lived in the apartment right below Dad's. Gloria answered and gave us each a kiss on the cheek. "These are for you," I said, handing her the flowers.

She bent her face toward the buds. "These smell exquisite," she said. "And look—they match me."

She was wearing a yellow dress, and seemed totally delighted by the coincidence, which made me happy, too.

"Chloe said yellow flowers mean friendship," Dad told her.

"I love that," Gloria said. "We're friends already."

Dad put the bag of groceries on the kitchen counter, and Sage came over to hug him hello. She was taller than me, not surprising for somebody my age. She came up to Dad's shoulder. "Good to see you again, kiddo," he said, mussing her hair.

"You too," she told him.

I said hi to Sage, and she said hi to me. I complimented her skirt, and she said thank you. Then I wasn't sure what to say next. I didn't know what we had in common, if anything, and we didn't have any history together. Sometimes making friends is harder work than it should be.

"Anyone want a drink?" Gloria asked. "There's seltzer and juice, and Jim, there's something for you on the back counter."

Dad went for the bottle of wine. "This is my favorite vintage," he said.

"I know," Gloria said with a smile. "Uncork it for us. I'll put Chloe's flowers in water."

I watched as he pulled open a drawer to get the bottle opener, and then took four glasses down from a high shelf above the stove. Sage and I got seltzer with a splash of cranberry juice in our glasses, and Dad poured wine into the other two. "To new friends," he said, clicking his glass with each of ours.

"To new friends," we all echoed.

We started dinner a few minutes later. Lemon chicken is pretty easy to prepare—especially with four people. Sage stepped up to the counter. "I call not chopping the onion," she said.

"Don't worry," Gloria said. "I'll take one for the team on onion duty."

"I can do it," I said. "I have a trick to keep from crying. Do you have any gum?"

"I think there's some on the back counter," Dad told me. He reached for it and handed it over. I popped a piece into my mouth, picked up a knife, and began slicing, tear-free.

"Wow, where'd you learn that?" Gloria asked.

"One of my dad's cooking magazines."

"You read cooking magazines, Jim," Gloria said. "Really?"

"When I'm not reading about more macho things, like cars and sporting events."

"That's not true," I said. "He only has magazines about cooking and being a dentist."

"Leave it to my daughter to keep me honest."

"Well, that's all perfectly legitimate reading material for a man—or a woman," Gloria said. "I just didn't know you did. You learn something new every day."

"It's really not hurting your eyes?" Sage asked me.

"Nope," I said.

"Can I try?"

"Of course."

Sage took the knife from me. She popped a piece of gum in her mouth and started chopping. "Wow, you're totally right," she said. "It's not bothering my eyes at all."

I looked at Dad and he winked at me. Then he turned back to the stove to heat oil in a saucepan. He added some wine (not his favorite vintage—that wine was too good to cook with, he explained), lemon juice, and a bunch of different spices. Gloria placed the chicken cutlets on a baking sheet, skin-side up, and told me to brush the sauce on them. I opened the drawer where Dad had found the bottle opener, but didn't see a basting brush.

"Where's the—" I started to ask.

"One drawer over," Dad said. "To your left."

I opened the drawer and, lo and behold, there was the brush. "Wow, Jimbo, you're like a psychic tonight," I told him.

"A man of many talents," Gloria said.

"All right, Chlo," Dad said. "Baste away."

I did, and Sage sprinkled salt and pepper on top of the chicken. Everything went into the oven. Gloria tossed the salad, and Dad made the dressing—but he kept it on the side for now, so the lettuce wouldn't get too soggy while we were waiting for the chicken to cook. We sat down together in the den.

"You have a faraway look in your eyes," Dad told Gloria. "What are you thinking about?"

"Just how lucky we are, to be here all together right now."

"That's what I'm thinking, too," Dad said. "Exactly." He was looking at Gloria in a way I'd never seen him look at another person—a small smile on his lips and a twinkle in his eye. Even before he and Mom had split, he'd never given her a look like that. At least not that I'd seen.

And suddenly it hit me like a ton of bricks. Why Gloria knew what Dad's favorite wine was, and how Dad knew where the wine opener and the basting brush were. Why Gloria was so interested in what magazines Dad read, and why Dad had wanted me to meet the Tofskys so badly to begin with. He and Gloria were dating.

Mom and Dad had only just split up. Sometimes at night I'd pass by Mom's bedroom and hear her sniffling, and I knew she was crying about it. It always made something drop in my stomach, and I'd feel a little bit sick, knowing Mom was really sad and there was nothing I could do about it.

Meanwhile, Dad already had a new girlfriend.

I'd even given Gloria yellow roses. I never would've even known what they meant if it hadn't been for Mom. Lia and I had made paper roses for Mother's Day, and we'd looked up on the Internet what the different colors meant. Our moms got pink-painted flowers for love and gratitude.

It seemed like a nice gesture, to give Gloria the color that meant friendship. But now it just seemed wrong. Like I'd been unfair to Mom somehow. I hadn't done it on purpose. I'd only been trying to be a good guest. For the first time in my entire life, it felt like being a good guest made me not such a good daughter. Even though Mom wasn't there to see, it made me feel really guilty.

At dinner, Dad sat next to Gloria, and Sage grabbed the seat on the other side of him. I sat across from Dad, but I couldn't really see him because Gloria had placed the flowers in the center of the table and they blocked my view.

"This is delicious," Gloria said. "We should do this more often."

"I'm sure that can be arranged," Dad told her.

"Hey, Jim, guess what," Sage said. "I did the high dive today."

"That's incredible," Dad said. He held up a hand and high-fived her. "It's sixteen feet—Chloe asked the lifeguard."

When Dad had first moved to the condo, we'd gone to the pool behind the building and he'd dared me to jump off the high dive. I dared him back. But neither of us was brave enough to take the dare.

"I'm really proud of you," Dad told Sage, sounding like a dad. I mean, sounding like he was *Sage's* dad. Bad enough that he was replacing Mom so fast. Now it felt like he'd found a new-and-improved daughter.

I guess if he wanted to be with Gloria instead of Mom, it made sense that he'd want to be around Gloria's daughter, too.

"Maybe tomorrow you can show Chloe and me how it's done," Dad told her.

"Sure!"

I pushed uneaten pieces of chicken around my plate. "Do you see your dad every other weekend?" I asked Sage.

"He lives in California," she said. "I see him on vacations."

"Oh."

Dad kicked me under the table and peeked around the flowers to give me a Look, even though I wasn't trying to be rude. I just wanted to know. Then Dad changed the subject, to the Billy Goat Trail, a hiking trail a patient of his had told him about. It turned out to be the Tofskys' favorite. "Oh, really," Dad said. "I'd love to try it." Even though in my whole life I'd never heard about Dad wanting to hike anything. Then Sage said there was one particularly steep part that most people walked around, but she climbed right up it. The way Dad reacted, you'd think Sage was the only person in the whole world ever to do such a thing.

Everyone had pretty much finished eating by then, so I stood to clear the table. "Oh, Chloe, you are a dear one," Gloria said. "Why don't you help her, Sage?"

Sage did, but I made sure to reach for Dad's plate first. "You know what I just remembered," he said, as he handed his plate over. "A couple years ago, Chloe had her friend Lia over for dinner. At the end of the meal, Emily asked Chloe to clear the table."

Sage had turned toward him, not really helping me, just listening. "Who's Emily?" she asked.

"Chloe's mom," Dad told her. He said it dismissively, like it didn't actually matter who Emily was. "Anyway, Chloe said no to helping. Apparently her friend Lia never had to. So I told Chloe, 'That's fine for you not to help clean up. But you should know if you're sitting there, I feel a song coming on.'"

"Did you actually start singing?" Sage asked.

"I didn't have to," Dad said. "The threat of her friend hearing me sing was enough to get Chloe to stand up and clear that table"—he snapped his fingers—"like that!"

"It was the one time in my whole life I didn't clean things up right away," I said.

"I wouldn't mind if you sang," Sage said.

"Yeah, you would," I told her. "You don't know him well enough to know this, but my dad has a voice like a dying cat." That's what Mom always said, anyway. I turned to Gloria. "You should know that."

"I consider myself duly warned," she said, and she added her plate to the pile in my hands.

"Thanks, Chlo," Dad said. "You're the best." He threw me a grin like everything was normal and great.

But I was thinking about Mom, and couldn't smile back.

CHAPTER 4

The next day was Sunday and Dad and I headed back to
Mom's house. Mom always dropped me off at Dad's condo,
and Dad always did the ride back to Mom's. That way they
both had to spend the same amount of time shuttling me
back and forth in the car.

The ride takes about a half hour. Dad used the time to talk
about the Tofskys, and how it was too bad it'd been drizzling
all day, so we'd missed seeing Sage on the high dive. Pretty
soon the condo association would be closing the pool for the
season, so we might not get the chance till next spring.

"It's okay," I said. I paused, then added, "To be honest, I
didn't like Sage that much."

"Really?" Dad asked. "Why?"

I shrugged my shoulders.

"Chloe?"

"I don't know. It's just a feeling I got. You think we should be friends just because we're the same age. But we didn't have anything else in common. I don't expect you to be friends with every single forty-two-year-old I meet."

"You meet a lot of forty-two-year-olds?" Dad asked.

"Maybe all of my new teachers will be forty-two years old."

"Then I'll be friends with them," Dad said. "My new friendships might be good for your grades."

"That'd be cheating," I told him.

"It was a joke, Chlo." I'd known that, of course, but I didn't say so.

"You want us to be friends just because Gloria is your girlfriend now," I said. When he didn't reply, I went on. "You can just admit that she is. It's totally obvious."

Dad sighed. "I wish you'd give Sage a chance, bear. She's a great girl. Gloria says Sage misses her dad a lot, and that has made her insecure."

"She didn't sound insecure when she talked about what a good hiker and diver she is."

"I think she wants us to like her, that's all," Dad said. "It's tough for Sage, having parents who live across the country from each other. You're lucky Mom and I are only a car ride apart."

"I don't feel lucky that you and Mom are a car ride apart."

We lapsed into silence. Dad made the right turn onto Parrott Drive. Mom's house was the second from the corner. Our old house had four bedrooms, and this one only had two. The kitchen was smaller, and our dining room table was pushed up against the wall in the living room. But those weren't the things I minded.

Dad shifted the car into "Park," but he left the engine running. "Well, bear," he said.

"Why don't you come in?" I asked. "You've never seen my room. You can't even see it from here. It's on the other side, facing the backyard. I set Captain Carrot's cage by the window, so he can enjoy the view. There's a big tree right there, so he stays nice and shady. Plus sometimes there are other rabbits on the lawn for him to look at."

"I don't think Mom would appreciate my coming in."

"You don't know that," I said. "Maybe she *wants* you to say hi. You were married to each other after all—for twelve and three-quarters *years*."

"I was there," Dad said. "I remember."

I looked away from him, toward the house that he'd never stepped inside. When Mom and Dad first told me they were splitting up, I didn't realize that meant I'd have to move. But they said our house was too big for just Mom and me to stay in, not to mention too expensive. Now there's another family living there. With their favorite foods in the fridge, and their pictures on the walls, and their friends hanging out in the den when they come over to visit.

Sometimes it feels like when something is over, it never counted in the first place.

"Don't you ever miss her?" I asked Dad, turning back to face him. "Don't you miss *us*?"

I meant us as a family. But Dad didn't understand that. "I miss you, bear," he said. "Of course I miss you."

He twisted to give me a peck on the cheek. I knew that meant it was time for me to go. Plus, I knew Mom was waiting on the other side of the door. Even though I couldn't see her, I could sense her there.

"'Bye," I said. "I miss you too."

CHAPTER 5

I woke up the next morning thinking about the bright side of being the new kid in school: you have a fresh chance to be whoever you want to be.

Obviously my first choice would be to have two parents who still lived in the same house and Lia right across the street, so we could walk to the first day of fifth grade together.

But the truth was, at the end of fourth grade it was only Lia who'd started being friends with Trissa Thompson. Trissa, along with her best friend Bianca DeLuca, invited Lia to be part of their club, the A-Team. When I asked Lia about my joining too, she said it wasn't really possible because I didn't have a letter *a* at the end of my first name. In fact, there wasn't an *a* at all in Chloe Michelle Silver. Which wasn't my fault. It's not like kids have any say in what their parents name them. If it had been up to me, I would've named myself Alana, which had not one *a*, not two, but three!

I got dressed and walked over to Captain Carrot's cage. "Hey, Cappy," I said, slipping a hand in to pet him. I ran my finger down the length of his white-and-brown speckled back. His fur was soft as cotton balls. "What do you think school will be like today? Will Monroe and Rachael remember me from Friday? I hope so. I hope my affirmation works."

Cappy nibbled my pinky finger. "I have the best friends in my new school. I have the best friends in my new school. I have the best friends in my new school," I said. My voice was super soft, but I knew he could hear me. Rabbits can hear up to two miles away. That's why their ears are so big.

"Chloe!" Mom called.

I scooped my brush and a hair tie off my dresser and headed downstairs. Mom had set a bowl of cornflakes out for me. "Good morning," I said. "Can you french braid my hair?"

"We're already low on time," Mom said. "I don't want either of us to be late for our first day."

"Please," I said. "I think it's how everyone wears it. I want to fit in here."

"Oh, Chloe," Mom said. Her voice was suddenly thick, like she was so sad she might even start crying. "I'm sorry about all the changes. I'm sorry for both of us."

"It's going to be okay," I quickly assured her. "I met nice kids the other day, and Regan Halliday is already your friend."

"That's right," she said, and she scooted behind me. "Okay. You eat, I'll braid."

"Thanks, Mom."

I dipped my head toward the bowl of cornflakes, but she pulled it back up again. "I'm going to give you a few dollars to keep in your backpack, in case something unexpected comes up."

"Like what?"

"If I knew that, then it wouldn't be unexpected," Mom said. "And remember when you get home—"

"I know, I know," I said. "When I get home, I call you at the office before I do anything else."

"That's right. Do not pass Go. Do not collect two hundred dollars. And if you need anything, you call Mrs. Wallace."

Mrs. Wallace was one of our new down-the-street neighbors. She ran a daycare business out of her house. Mom had agreed with me that I was too old to spend the two hours between the end of the school day and when she got home after work with a bunch of toddlers in Mrs. Wallace's living room. But she'd arranged it with her to be an emergency contact for me.

"Her number is on the fridge," Mom said.

"I know."

"Good," Mom said. "Hand me the hair tie."

"Are you done?"

"Yeah."

I turned to face her. "How does it look?"

"The braid looks okay. The kid is spectacular."

A half hour later, I was at Ms. Danos's classroom door. Ms. Danos herself was standing in the doorframe when I walked up. I told her my name, she checked it against her list, and then pointed out the seat in the third row that was mine. As I walked past, Lucy Tanaka waved to me from her seat in the first row. I waved back.

"Hey, Chloe," Monroe called.

"Hi!" I said. I dropped my backpack at my seat and unzipped the front pocket. I'd stuck a pocket mirror in there. It was the shape of the sun, and it had been a party favor at Lia's younger sister's birthday party the year before. I palmed it and quickly checked my braid to make sure it looked okay. Then I headed over to where Monroe was, sitting at a desk in the back row, another girl standing next to her.

"Good, you wore a french braid," Monroe said. She had one herself, too. "This is Anjali," she went on, pointing toward the other girl, also in a braid.

"Nice to meet you," I said. "I'm Chloe."

"Obvi," Anjali said.

"Well, the gang's all here now," Monroe said.

"Except Rachael. Can you believe she's in Mr. Goldfarb's class by herself?" Anjali asked.

"It's better than being a hundred miles away like Haley," Monroe said. She turned to me. "Our friend Haley moved away over the summer."

"Like I did," I said.

"Yeah, but you're lucky," Monroe said. "You met us."

Dad had said I was lucky, too. But when Monroe said it, I actually agreed with her.

"You'll sit with us at lunch today, okay?" she asked.

"Okay," I said, grinning. "Thanks."

The bell rang a couple minutes later, and Anjali and I scrambled to our desks. Mine was by the window. On the other side of me was a boy scribbling notes in a spiral note-book. When he caught me looking at him, he shielded his book like we were taking a test and I was trying to copy him.

"Welcome to the first day of fifth grade!" Ms. Danos said.

The morning passed by in a blur, and before I knew it, it was lunchtime. I went to check in with Mr. Dibble, like he'd asked me to. He wasn't there, so I left my name with the receptionist. By the time I got to the lunchroom, there was a long, winding line to get food. I got a plate of ravioli and was about to head to the utensil area when there was a huge *SMASH* behind me. I turned to see Lucy Tanaka. Her tray of food was on the floor (and partially on her clothes). "Oops, not again!" Lucy said.

"Sorry, sorry," said the boy who sat beside me in Ms. Danos's class. His tray was also on the floor, but he seemed more concerned with the splashes of spaghetti sauce on his textbook, which he wiped with his sleeve.

"It's a bit of a hazard to read while balancing a tray of pasta in your arms," Lucy said. But she didn't sound mad.

I set down my tray by the salad bar and grabbed a fistful of napkins. "Here, let me help," I said.

"Chloe to the rescue—for a second time!" Lucy said. "Thank you!"

"No problem," I said. "By the way, my mom puts baking soda on stains. I could ask if they have some, if you want."

"This sauce comes out in the wash," Lucy said. She slid her eyes toward the boy. "We know from experience, right, Theo?"

Theo muttered in agreement—or disagreement, it was hard to tell. Other kids stepped around, while the three of us got things mostly cleaned up. "Do you guys want to sit together for lunch?" Lucy asked.

Theo tucked his book under his arm. "I have work to do," he said.

"And I—" I started, but then I cut myself off, because Monroe was crossing the room toward us.

"I was beginning to think you got lost," she told me.

"There was just a little accident," I explained.

"Things look okay now, though. We've been saving a seat for you."

"Cool, thanks." I turned to Lucy. "Do you want to sit with us?"

"The table's full," Monroe cut in. "Except for the seat we saved for you, of course."

"Oh, I'm sorry."

"It's okay," Lucy said. "Maybe we can eat together another time."

"Sure," I said. I grabbed my tray off the countertop.

"Wait a sec," Monroe said. "You're not eating *that*, are you?"

"Yeah," I said. "Why?"

"Oh, Chloe, I have so much to teach you," she said, shaking her head in a tsk-tsk grown-up kind of way. "Like how no one eats the hot food. It's practically a law."

"I eat the hot food, and I've never been arrested," Lucy said.

Monroe ignored her. "I'll take you to get a sandwich," she told me.

"Um. Okay." I turned to Lucy. "Do you want my ravioli? Since yours spilled, and that way it won't go to waste. I swear I didn't touch it yet."

"Sure, thanks again," Lucy said.

Monroe swept a finger through the air and circled in on Lucy. "So, are you dressed as a lizard or something?"

With the crash and the cleanup I'd barely noticed what Lucy was wearing. But now I looked at her and saw what Monroe was seeing: a black T-shirt underneath a shiny green vest, and pants that matched. To be honest, it did look a bit lizard-y.

"I found my brother's old dragon Halloween costume," Lucy said.

"I think 'Halloween' is the key word," Monroe said. "Ready to go, Chloe?"

"Um, sure."

She led me to a counter in the back with bread and cold cuts. I made a turkey sandwich, because that's what Monroe said she had made for herself, and then we headed to a table in the back where Rachael and Anjali were waiting for us.

"Chloe is so lucky that Dibble assigned me to show her around," Monroe said, settling into her seat. "I just rescued her from the grips of Theo Barnes and Lucy Tanaka."

"Oooh," Rachael said. "What were you doing with them?"

"Theo accidentally knocked Lucy's tray," I said. "I helped clean it up."

"I saw you waving at Lucy this morning," Anjali said. "Are you friends or something?"

"I'm not really friends with anyone," I said. *I have the best friends in my new school.* "I mean, not yet."

"But were you popular at your old school?"

I thought about Trissa, and Bianca, and Lia, too, and I felt my cheeks start to warm up. "Oh, yeah," I said quickly. "I was."

"Of course she was," Monroe said. "I told you, Chloe's cool. She didn't know any better about Lucy and Theo, because I hadn't had a chance to tell her everything. But just so you know, Chloe, they're just about the last people you'd want to be friends with—and for good reason."

"Reasons," Anjali corrected. "Plural. For one thing, Theo is a total know-it-all."

"And he wouldn't want to be friends with you anyway," Rachael added. "He prefers books to people."

"He bumped into Lucy because he was reading a book," I said.

"You see what I mean!" Monroe said. "And you saw what Lucy was wearing." She turned to the other girls: "a lizard costume!"

Rachael shook her head, laughing.

"I think she dresses that way because she doesn't have a mom at home," Anjali said.

"Her mom died," Rachael filled in for me.

"That's so sad," I said.

"It is," Monroe agreed. "But Lucy's grandmother lives with them now. My grandmother would never let me wear a Halloween costume on a regular school day."

"Not that I'd ever want to," Anjali said.

"If Lucy had her way, you would," Monroe said. "She's so pushy about it. Remember when we were all in Brownies in second grade and we had those patches? She added more to her sash until she had too many to fit, so she sewed them onto a vest that she wore every day."

"Like a patch with bells on it?" I asked.

"Exactly. How'd you know?"

"I heard you guys talking about it on Book Pickup Day."

"I hate to admit it, but I wore the Brownie patches, too," Anjali said. "We all did."

"You wore the *official* patches," Monroe said. "So did I. Actually I had the most—because I earned them. But then Lucy started making up her own. A patch for loving macaroni and cheese, a patch for doing jumping jacks. You could tell they were fake because they were completely unprofessional. The edges were all frayed. She practically forced everyone to make their own patches up, too. She always tries to get people to change their style to her weird style." She paused to take a breath. "My point is, Chloe, if you get too close to her, you might end up in a lizard costume."

I squirmed in my seat a bit. It's not that I'd want to wear a lizard costume. But the patch thing didn't seem so bad. In fact, it seemed like maybe Lucy was trying to be nice and include people. I certainly didn't want to make fun of her for it—especially after hearing what had happened to her mom.

"Is there anything else I need to know about Braywood?" I asked. *Please, please, don't let it be about Lucy.*

"Oh, tons," Monroe said. "First off, Daniel Carson is the cutest boy in school."

"And he's in *my* class," Rachael said.

I breathed a sigh of relief as Monroe went on—that Jesse Freeman in our class was second cutest, that the only acceptable day to eat the hot food was Taco Day, and that I should never use the bathroom at the end of the hall on the first floor, because the air vent went to the library.

"You can hear everything!" Anjali exclaimed.

"Gross," I said.

"Plus, there's Dr. Garcia," Monroe said. "He teaches science and he's the oldest teacher in the school by about a hundred years. He sleeps through most of class himself. You don't learn anything, but you get to sit with your friends—so obviously you'll sit with us."

"And another thing," said Rachael. "Danos and Goldfarb are secretly dating."

"That's just a rumor," Anjali said.

"Rumors can be true," Rachael said. "This one definitely is. I saw them holding hands in the hall this morning."

"You did not," Monroe said.

"I did! They passed each other in the hall and they brushed their hands up against each other—like *purposefully*."

Monroe rolled her eyes. "Rachael thinks everything is some kind of love story. She loves romantic things."

"Because her parents are divorced," Anjali added.

"Mine are, too," I said.

"Is that why you switched schools?"

"Yeah. My mom moved here, to Braywood, and my dad moved to a condo closer to his office."

"So you live with your mom?" Monroe asked.

"Except every other weekend when I'm at my dad's," I said. "And also Wednesday nights."

"My parents both live in Braywood, and I live with them the exact same amount," Rachael said. "I do two days with my mom, and two days with my dad, and then back to my mom's."

"It's totally confusing," Anjali said.

"Not really," Rachael said. "On 'A' weeks I'm with my dad Monday, Tuesday, Friday, and Saturday, and on 'B' weeks—"

"Forget it," Monroe broke in. "We're never going to remember."

"It's not that hard," Rachael said, but softly, more to herself than anyone else.

"Can I ask you a question?" I asked her.

"You just did," she said. "But you can ask another."

"Is your dad dating anyone?"

She shook her head. "I'm pretty sure he's still in love with my mom, and she's still in love with him. I think maybe they just needed a little break, but lately when they look at each other, they give each other . . . I don't know how to explain it . . . like googly-eyed looks."

I knew what she meant, because I'd seen Dad give that kind of look to Gloria. It made me jealous that Rachael's parents looked that way at each other, even if they were divorced, too.

"If they get remarried, I mean to each other, I'll be a junior bridesmaid," Rachael went on.

"You could be one even if they got remarried to other people," Monroe said.

"I don't think that's possible," Rachael told her. "Anyway, Chloe, do you have more questions about school?"

"Umm . . . ," I started. I'd had so many questions for Captain Carrot that morning. But now that there were three people in front of me ready and able to answer them, they seemed to have all flown out of my head. "What about summer reading? Did you write up book reports?"

"Oh, you don't have to do that," Monroe said. "I didn't even read anything. The teachers assign summer reading as a way to trick you into doing work. They never actually check to see if you did. Another reason why you're really lucky Dibble paired us up, for me to tell you these things." She paused, then added, "There's one more thing I have to tell you." Her eyes flicked quickly to the two other girls. Anjali and Rachael each gave little nods of their heads. "We have a club called the It Girls. I'm the president, because it was my idea. It's a really exclusive club—the most exclusive in the fifth grade, and maybe in the whole school. We always have lunch together, and we have meetings after school twice a week."

The It Girls sounded a lot like the A-Team. Except I wouldn't be excluded from it. That's why she was telling me about it, I was sure: because she wanted me to be in it. My heart started to beat faster in excitement.

"We've always had four members," Monroe went on. "Then Haley moved away. We've had a bunch of meetings to discuss who could replace her. Would you be interested?"

"Oh, definitely!" I practically shouted. "Count me in!"

"Hang on," Rachael said. "It's not that easy."

"Lots of people are interested," Anjali said. "We can't let them all in."

"Right," Monroe said. "You seem like the kind of person who would fit in our club, but it's a big decision that we need to make carefully. Since you're interested in joining, we'll have a trial period. That's a club rule, when we're considering a new member. You can eat lunch with us, and come to our meetings, and we'll decide if you're the right fit."

"How long does the trial last?" I asked.

"However long we decide it to be."

"And then I'm in?"

"Keep being cool," Monroe told me. "And you will be."

CHAPTER 6

According to the schedule I'd gotten on Book Pickup Day, we were supposed to have science with Dr. Garcia three times a week—the last two periods of the day on Mondays, Wednesdays, and Fridays.

At one thirty-five on the dot, Ms. Danos walked us down to the science lab for seventh period. I'd pictured Dr. Garcia as an old man with a long white beard and the wrinkly kind of eyes, but when we got there, it was Mr. Dibble behind the teacher's desk. "Come in! Come in!" he called to us. "Your names are at your seats!"

Instead of desks arranged around the room, there were eight tables with black countertops. Two side-by-side, going back four rows. Each had room for three students. Someone—probably Mr. Dibble himself—had placed a small square of paper at each seat, like the place cards my aunt Louise had at her wedding.

My name was in the back row. Anjali and Monroe were two rows in front of me, with a boy named Huck sitting in between them. My seat was between Lucy Tanaka and Theo Barnes.

"Hi, Chloe!" Lucy said, plopping into the seat next to mine.

"Hey," I said. "How was the ravioli?"

"Delicious," she said. "Thanks."

"You're welcome."

Lucy leaned across me. "Hi, Theo," she said. "Look at us—it's like a lunchtime reunion!"

"We didn't sit together at lunch," Theo mumbled. He put his arms protectively over the books he'd placed in front of him.

"Huck, trade seats with Chloe," Monroe said. She'd twisted around in her seat to look at me, and I stood and picked up my place card right away.

"Sorry," I told Lucy. "I guess I have to go." A couple rows in front of me, I saw Huck standing and picking his place card up, too.

"Hey, Harper," another kid called. "Will you trade seats with me?"

"Jesse, trade with me!"

There was a flurry of activity, but then Mr. Dibble put two fingers in his mouth and whistled the loudest whistle ever, which stopped all of us in our tracks.

"How'd you do that?" Huck asked.

"Find me at lunchtime tomorrow, Mr. Fox, and I'll teach you," Mr. Dibble said. "As long as you promise not to use the skill inside a classroom—like I did just now."

"Deal," Huck said.

"And no trading seats, all right?"

"All right."

"Excuse me, Mr. Dibble," Monroe said.

"Yes, Ms. Reeser?"

"I heard that Dr. Garcia lets kids pick their own seats. Anjali and I were planning to have Chloe Silver sit with us. Remember, you're the one who said I should show her around school."

"Oh, yes, Ms. Silver," Mr. Dibble said, noticing me in the back for the first time. "I got a note from you this morning."

"At lunchtime," I corrected. "You said to check in."

"That's right. Well, it's good to see you've made some friends already. And, Ms. Reeser, I appreciate that you have taken your job as tour guide so seriously. But it'll be good for Ms. Silver to branch out and sit with some of her other classmates. Please, everyone, take your seats."

I sat back down, in the seat between Theo and Lucy, and stared at the back of Monroe's head, hoping this didn't count against me in my trial period. I would've switched seats if I could have, but I didn't have any choice. She had to understand that.

Then again, I didn't have any choice about my name, and that didn't matter to the A-Team.

"So," Mr. Dibble said, "I know you're all wondering where Dr. Garcia is, and I'm sorry to report—"

"He's dead?" a girl named Isabelle guessed.

"No, of course he's not dead," Mr. Dibble said. "He decided to retire. A bit earlier than we'd expected, but it's not undeserved. Dr. Garcia was a teacher at this school for fifty-seven years."

A bunch of kids gasped when Mr. Dibble said that—fifty-seven years. I wondered why anyone thought his retirement was unexpected.

"But I'm very happy to be here with you," Mr. Dibble went on, and he sounded like a kid who'd just opened a bunch of presents on Christmas morning. "Science was my favorite subject in school. Any questions so far?"

Theo raised his hand, and Mr. Dibble called on him. "Have you ever actually taught science before?" Theo asked.

"The honest answer is, no I have not. I do have Dr. Garcia's excellent notes to follow." Mr. Dibble tapped a pile in front of him. "And I remember what *I* learned in fifth-grade science quite well. So let's get started, shall we? Who can tell me the steps of the scientific method?"

Theo was the only one who raised his hand, and when Mr. Dibble called on him, I opened up the green notebook I picked for science class—green because it seemed like a science kind of color. So far the pages inside were blank, which is how I like them best, before I've crossed things out, or doodled in the margins. It's so clean and fresh, and when you look at them it feels like everything you write will turn out neat and perfect.

Theo rattled off the steps, and I wrote them down in my best handwriting: (1) Ask a question, (2) Do background research, (3) State your hypothesis, (4) Conduct an experiment to test it, (5) Analyze the data and draw a conclusion, and (6) Write up your results.

"Good job," Mr. Dibble said. "Now, uh, who can tell me what a hypothesis is?"

No one raised a hand except Theo—again. Mr. Dibble seemed to look around the room for someone else, anyone else, before he said, "Yes, Mr. Barnes?"

"A hypothesis is a proposed explanation that may serve as the starting point for further exploration," Theo said.

"Huh?" Monroe asked, without raising her hand.

"Okay, let's unpack that," Mr. Dibble said. "Let's say for example you are wondering whether . . . whether people with different eye colors have different kinds of taste buds. In my family, my wife and I love broccoli, but our children do not. My wife and I both have brown eyes, and our kids have blue eyes. So my hypothesis would be that overall, people with brown eyes have more of a taste for green vegetables. Now how might I conduct that experiment?"

A few more kids raised their hands. I half listened to the answer, and I half thought about my own taste buds, and how a turkey sandwich was not exactly my favorite lunch, but it seemed that eating what Monroe thought I should eat instead of eating ravioli would help me to become an It Girl. That was my own, private hypothesis. I'd conduct the experiment each day. I hoped the results would be what I wanted them to be. My stomach flip-flopped just thinking about it, and I repeated my affirmation in my head:

I have the best friends in my new school. I have the best friends in my new school. I have the best friends in my new school.

At the end of class, Mr. Dibble dismissed us without any homework. I said good-bye to Lucy and Theo, grabbed my books, and hurried toward the front of the room, to catch up to my new friends.

CHAPTER 7

"CHLOE! BREAKFAST!" Mom called the next morning.

I grabbed my brush and a hair tie, and headed into the kitchen. As soon as I sat down at the table, Mom stood behind me to braid. "I think I'm getting better at eating while you're braiding," I told her. "I haven't dripped any milk."

"We're quite a team," she said, as she yanked a clump of my hair tighter. I stifled the word *ow* in my throat because I didn't want to hurt her feelings. "At least one of my jobs is going well."

"There's something wrong at Regan Halliday's office?" I asked.

"I'm having trouble with the filing system," Mom said. "I'm only about twenty percent on top of it. Maybe fifteen percent."

"But weren't you in charge of the filing system at Dad's office?" I said.

"I designed that one," Mom said. "I never thought I'd have to learn another. But then, I never thought things would turn out the way they did with your dad."

She said the word "dad" like she'd just tasted milk gone sour. Worse than that, actually. Like she didn't want to say his name at all. It was like Dad was her version of Lord Voldemort in a Harry Potter book. I made a deal with myself right then: I wouldn't mention Dad to Mom again, unless it was absolutely necessary.

"Hey, you want to know what Lia told me last night," I said, trying to change the subject. "The Thompson family got a dog."

"That's nice," Mom said "All good in Lia's world?"

"Mmm hmm," I said. I didn't tell her that Lia hadn't been able to talk long, since she was meeting Trissa and Bianca (and Trissa's new dog) at Magic Cone. She said they'd gone a bunch of times, and they shared three flavors between them. Of course I told her about being in the It Girls Club. I said it like I was already part of it, not to lie, but because that's what Erin Lindstrom did: when she wanted something to happen, she said it like it already had.

Mom reached out a hand. I handed her the hair tie, and she twisted it around the bottom. "There you go. All done. Now you better get a move on, and I should, too."

"I hope you have a good day," I told her.

"You too, sweetheart," she said.

I walked into Ms. Danos's class just as she was closing the classroom door and starting the day's first lesson. When I glanced to the back, I saw Monroe's hair was hanging loose, down past her shoulders. Ms. Danos asked everyone to open their math books to page fourteen. Down the row, Anjali was flipping her book open. Her hair was loose, too, and the dark curtain of it obscured her face so I couldn't meet her eye. Maybe french braids were only required on the first day of school and optional every other day. But at lunchtime Monroe set me straight: "It Girls only wear braids on previously agreed upon special occasions. A random Tuesday is definitely not a french braid day."

"I'm so sorry," I told her.

"It's okay because you didn't know," she said. "As long as you take it out now."

She barely had the sentence out of her mouth before I'd undone the elastic from the bottom of the braid and slipped it onto my wrist like a bracelet, and unraveled my hair quick as possible.

The hot lunch that day was some sort of chicken dish, but we bypassed the line and went to the sandwich station. Rachael's class had gotten out a couple minutes before ours. She was sitting at the same table in the back when we got there with our turkey sandwiches. Her hair was in a half ponytail.

"This afternoon will be the first official It Girls meeting of fifth grade," Monroe said, taking the seat next to Rachael. "I assume you're free for this, Chloe?"

"Of course I am," I said.

"Good."

"Will we meet at your house, like usual?" Rachael asked her.

"My mom has to run lines, so . . ." Monroe shrugged instead of finishing the sentence.

"Run lines?" I asked.

"She's rehearsing," Monroe said.

"Her mom's an actress," Anjali added.

"That's so cool! Would I have seen her movies?"

"She's not in movies," Rachael said. "Or TV shows."

"Only because she's a *stage* actress," Monroe said. "Which is a much harder kind of actress to be. You're in front of a live audience every night, and if you make a mistake, they can't just tape the scene again."

"Wow," I said.

"She was in a vitamin commercial, too," Anjali said. Her voice changed to a mock-announcer voice: "take two, and you *won't* have to call your doctor in the morning."

"Wow," I said again. "I know that commercial. I totally saw her. She looks a lot like you. Or you look a lot like her."

"Do you really think so?"

"Totally."

"Thanks," Monroe said. "Anyway, it's really hard work, what my mom does. She has to be perfect. She doesn't like to have people around when she's trying to memorize a bunch of dialogue."

"If you want, we could have the meeting at my house," I offered.

"That's great," Monroe said. "You're on."

If I'd known ahead of time that the It Girls would be coming to my house, I would've prepared for it. The breakfast dishes were still in the sink, and we didn't have much to eat besides cornflakes, plus the veggies and pasta that Mom had most likely bought for dinner. But it turned out to be fine, because everyone wanted to order pizza anyway.

I called Mom first, to let her know I was home. Then the other girls called their parents. Rachael was the last one to use the phone, and she hung up with her mother and dialed the pizza place. "What toppings does everyone want?" she asked, holding the ringing phone against her ear.

"Mushrooms," Monroe and I said at the same time.

"Ew," Anjali said. "Plain cheese."

"I know, I hate mushrooms," Rachael said.

"Fine," Monroe told them. "Get half plain for you guys, and half mushroom for us." She looked at me and grinned. "The better half," she said.

Rachael placed the order. With the soda and garlic knots everyone wanted, the total came to over thirty dollars. The other girls didn't have much money on them, but luckily I had a bunch saved up from my grandma Barb.

Grandma Barb is Dad's mother. She gives me money at the end of every school year, five dollars for every good grade, even though Mom always says she shouldn't, because Mom believes hard work is its own reward. If you get good grades, you can get into college—maybe even on scholarship. And if you work hard in college, you can get a good job when you graduate, and then you'll make your own money to buy what you want.

That seemed like an awfully long time to wait, but Grandma would always sneak me the money anyway. I supposed it would be a whole lot easier for her to do so now, since the split. So there was a bright side for you.

I had a hundred and sixty-seven dollars stashed in my top drawer, from what Grandma Barb had given me, plus my allowance and various birthday gifts from other relatives. I'd been saving up for something special—or a few something specials. Having the It Girls at my house certainly qualified, if you asked me. "I have plenty of money," I told them. "Pizza is my treat."

The food arrived and we ate it around the coffee table. Afterward we put on some music, like Lia and I used to do. Monroe choreographed a dance for us. We pushed the coffee table to the side of the room, and she told us to take our positions. Anjali was in front of me, but Monroe told her to step behind. "Mushroom lovers stage front!" she said.

I jumped forward, toward the TV. Monroe took my hand and swung it up, then we stepped back, and she told Anjali and Rachael to dip under us. There were hand movements, and more footwork. It wouldn't have worked with only three people, because some parts involved having partners, two and two. I felt like I belonged.

We practiced until we knew the dance by heart, and by then it was almost time for Mom to be home.

I stood at the front door as my new friends were leaving. "Thanks for coming," I called. "I hope we do it again."

Monroe turned to back to grin at me. "Absolutely," she said.

CHAPTER 8

"I have decided that this semester, you kids will help me with the lessons," Mr. Dibble said.

It was Wednesday afternoon, and we were back in science class. Theo was shaking his head. Other kids were shaking their heads, too. But I knew not for the same reason.

"Don't worry. You guys already know more than you think," Mr. Dibble said. "For example, the steps of the scientific method. Who remembers them?"

A few hands shot up. I flipped open my green notebook and raised my hand, too. "Ms. Silver," Mr. Dibble said.

I read out loud: "ask a question, do background research, make a hypothesis, perform an experiment, draw a conclusion, and write up your results."

"Excellent," Mr. Dibble said. "That's excellent."

Theo raised his hand, and Mr. Dibble called, "Yes, Mr. Barnes?"

"I'm not trying to be rude," Theo said. "But Chloe's just reading from her notes. What about the other things we're supposed to learn?"

"I bet *you* already know the other things we're supposed to learn," Lucy said.

Theo lowered his head. "I read. So sue me," he muttered, and a few kids snickered.

"Settle down," Mr. Dibble said. "It's a wonderful thing that Mr. Barnes reads as much as he does. And do you know why he does? Because he's curious. I want you *all* to have that curiosity. You're in fifth grade now, so you're old enough to understand a lot about the world. And you're also young enough to appreciate you still have a lot to figure out. I'll tell you a secret, the adults in your life don't have it all figured out, either. We just have a harder time admitting it."

"You just admitted it, though," Jesse pointed out.

"Yes, Mr. Freeman," Mr. Dibble agreed. "And I'll admit something else, too. Sometimes I don't even know what questions I'm supposed to ask. Sometimes I don't know what to be curious about. For example, until I started working here I didn't know that bacon would taste even better dipped into syrup. Then on Brunch for Lunch Day, I saw a couple kids in the cafeteria eating that very combination. A hypothesis popped up in my head: I bet mixing savory and sweet ingredients tastes good. I conducted my own experiment the next morning, and drew the conclusion that my hypothesis was correct."

"That's your second food example," Anjali said. "So are we going to be doing food experiments in class?"

"I'm glad you asked, Ms. Sheth. I'll tell you my plan. Every week or so, a different table will get together and come up with a question. It doesn't have to have anything to do with food. It *does* have to relate to your curiosity."

"I'm curious whether the Capitals will win the Stanley Cup this year," Huck called out.

"I am, too, believe me," Mr. Dibble said. "But that's a different kind of curiosity. It involves a lot of variables I don't control. I'm talking about the kind of question that when it occurs to you, you can get in there and research it for yourself, without sitting home and waiting by the television. Every law of science we have is because someone with a curious mind asked a question. Now you will do the same. Do the research, formulate a hypothesis, conduct an experiment, draw a conclusion, and report your findings to us. Doesn't that sound great?"

"You don't expect us to invent new laws of science, do you?" Monroe asked, which was the exact same thing I was thinking.

"People don't *invent* laws of science," Theo said. "They *discover* them."

"Know-it-all," Monroe said.

"Now, now," Mr. Dibble said. "I understand what you're getting at, Ms. Reeser. And the answer is, you don't know what you'll discover until you ask the questions."

"How do we know what the right questions are?" Harper asked.

"A little thing called observation," Mr. Dibble said. "Did you know gravity was discovered because Sir Isaac Newton observed an apple falling from a tree and became curious as to why? A single, solitary apple in his backyard sparked a question that led to the discovery of something that affects every person, in every town, in every country on our planet. Science is global. Isn't that exciting?"

We murmured that yes, it was.

"Think about the things you see and experience in the world, the things that make *you* curious," Mr. Dibble went on. "Ask a question and do the research. Conduct an experiment. You can be as creative as you'd like—there will be added points for creativity. I'm less concerned with the results than I am with the process. But who knows? You may just discover something that affects all our lives."

Next to me, Theo let out a little sound, so soft. "Whoa." When I looked over at him, he was smiling. Actually smiling. It made me realize I'd never seen him do that before.

"Now, I'm going to write down a number between one and a hundred," Mr. Dibble told us. "You should each pull out a sheet of paper and do the same."

I turned a page in my green notebook and wrote the number "4," for no other reason than my birthday is April fourth. Plus, four people is the perfect amount for a choreographed dance, and if I became an official It Girl, there'd be four people in the club again. Mr. Dibble told us all to hold up our numbers. He went around the room looking at them, and then announced our table would go first. "Mr. Barnes and I had the exact same number," he said.

He held opened his own notebook to show us: he and Theo had each written "1."

"So Mr. Barnes and his tablemates will go first," Mr. Dibble said.

Theo raised his hand and Mr. Dibble called on him. "I don't mind working alone," Theo said.

"No, this is a group exercise," Mr. Dibble told him. "Imagine how much you can discover if you harness the curiosity of *three* minds. Since you're the first group, I'll give you an extra half week. This will be due the Monday after next. How does that sound?"

"Great," Lucy said. She tapped my hand with the same kind of excitement in Mr. Dibble's voice.

"Fine," Theo said.

Monroe had twisted in her seat to look at me and gave me a shrug of sympathy. I gave her a little shrug back.

"Fine with me too," I said.

CHAPTER 9

Theo had suggested we get started that day. But Wednesday afternoons Lucy had a piano lesson right after school, and by the time she was done, I had to head to Dad's. To be perfectly honest, I was a bit relieved that the science project had to wait. I was thinking about that shrug Monroe had given me in science class. It's not that I minded working with Lucy and Theo, but it made me feel like I was caught in the middle of two sides—Lucy and Theo on one side, and Monroe and the It Girls on the other.

So being at Dad's seemed like a good break. At least until I got there. I'd hoped we could have a makeup Father/ Daughter Pizza Night, and maybe I'd talk to Dad about everything at school. But Dad had already made other plans, and those plans involved ordering in gluten-free Chinese food with Gloria and Sage.

Talk about being stuck in the middle—Mom on one side, and Gloria and Sage (and Dad) on the other.

The Tofskys arrived, and I didn't have time to sit in my seat or even leave my cup at my place setting to claim it before Sage had plopped herself down, right next to Dad. "Hey, Jim," she said. "Guess what. I'm going to be in my school play!"

"Good for you," Dad told her. "Chloe was in *Annie* at her school last year. She sang a couple lines in 'It's the Hard-Knock Life.' What part were you again, bear?"

"Orphan number four," I said. I'd tried out for Molly, one of the orphans who actually had a name, but Bianca DeLuca had gotten that role. Dad said it was okay, though. He said there were no small parts, just small actors.

"That's right," he said now. "What play are you doing, Sage?"

"*Alice in Wonderland*," she told him. "I'm going to be Alice."

"How spectacular!" he exclaimed. "Chloe, isn't that spectacular?"

I swallowed a bite of sweet-and-sour chicken. "Sure," I said.

"The audition was this morning," Sage said. "I did a monologue about when Alice chases the White Rabbit and falls down the hole."

"I'd love to see you perform it after dinner," Dad said.

Which of course meant that *I* had to see it, too. I have to admit, Sage was pretty good. She only had to glance at the script once, and the show wasn't even happening for a month.

But then Dad stood and gave her a standing ovation, and I knew he didn't really mean it when he said there were no small parts, because he thought it was an awfully big deal that Sage had the title role. I couldn't wait to get back to Mom's house.

⭐

I had an It Girls meeting on Thursday, so it wasn't until Friday that Lucy, Theo, and I got together to talk about our project for Mr. Dibble's class. We decided to go to Theo's house, because he practically had a library full of science books in his bedroom. He told us to observe things on our walk, to see if any discoveries popped out at us.

"I'm seeing cars and trees and houses," Lucy said. "And look—Vanessa Medina dropped a gum wrapper and it fell to the ground!"

I picked the wrapper up and threw it in the trash can on the corner. "Newton already discovered gravity," Theo told Lucy. "We need a question we don't know the answer to yet."

"*O-kay*. Have you ever thought about wearing colors besides white and tan?"

"The answer to that is it's not relevant," Theo said. "And besides, I don't think you're in the position to mock someone's clothes." At that moment, Lucy herself was wearing a cloak of about a thousand colors, which she'd told me was from when her brother had starred in his high school production of *Joseph and the Amazing Technicolor Dreamcoat*.

"I'm not mocking them at all," Lucy said. "Honestly. I was just curious."

"Well, I like my clothes," Theo said. "And we need to concentrate on *real* questions. Mr. Dibble just gave us a big opportunity. You guys need to take this seriously."

"I am taking it seriously," I told him.

"Me too," Lucy said.

"Good, because can you imagine how good it would look on our college applications if we actually *did* discover something new?" Theo asked.

"We have"—Lucy paused to count—"Seven years before we apply to college."

"It's never too early to start thinking about it," Theo said. "Plus, if we make a new discovery, we can probably skip a few years and go straight to Harvard. Or at least skip into sixth grade. Now I have some thoughts on chaos theory."

"What's chaos theory?" I asked.

"The study of nonlinear dynamics," Theo told me.

"What?"

"Any-hoo," Lucy cut in. "That's where I live. Right over there." She pointed out a gray clapboard house. "I'd invite you in to meet my grandma, but she's volunteering today. You guys should hold your breath."

"Why?" I asked.

"Because we're about to pass Mrs. Gallagher's house," Lucy said.

She'd stopped in her tracks. Her voice had dropped a couple decibels lower, and she nodded toward the house next door to her own. It was also gray; but unlike Lucy's house, you could tell it hadn't been painted that color. Instead, it was a very, very dirty white house. Two of the window shutters were hanging crooked, and the windows themselves were caked with dirt. The front yard was littered with sticks and leaves that looked like they'd been there for a few seasons.

"When I was little," Lucy said, "I used to think she was a witch, and I made up all sorts of rules. Like if I held my breath when I passed by, then I'd be immune to her spells."

"There are about a thousand problems with your logic," Theo said, stepping forward. "First of all, there's no such thing as witches. And second, even if there was, when you breathe you're inhaling molecules of everyone who ever lived. It's a scientific phenomenon called Caesar's last breath. So holding yours in front of her house won't do any good. You're getting her molecules anyway."

Just then, one of the dirt-caked windows was thrown open. "I see you kids on my lawn!" a crackly voice cried out. "You're a nuisance to the neighborhood! Your parents should know better than to let you wander alone. Get out of here before I—"

Lucy shrieked and the three of us took off down the block, not stopping until we'd turned the corner. We were panting and took a few seconds to catch our breaths.

"What'd you ever do to her?" Theo asked.

"Nothing, I swear," Lucy said. "Maybe we just discovered that witches really do exist!"

"A scientific impossibility," Theo told her.

"I'd still feel safer if she wasn't my next-door neighbor."

I patted Lucy's shoulder, feeling sad for her. "Hey, you know what I just discovered through my power of observation?" I asked.

"What?"

"The ice-cream truck," I said, pointing all the way down the block.

I still had the five dollars Mom had given me on Monday in my backpack, and I treated each of us to a vanilla cone. I held my ice cream in one hand, and with the other I dropped a penny from my change on the ground.

"You dropped your money," Theo told me, bending to pick it up.

"No, no, leave it," I said. "I did it on purpose."

"Why?"

"That way someone else can walk by and get lucky pennies," I explained, and I dropped another.

"That's so cool!" Lucy said.

"Lucky pennies are a scientific impossibility," Theo said.

"Hey!" a voice squealed from behind. The three of us turned to see a little boy. He looked about four years old. "Look! Mom! I'm finding treasure!"

"One man's scientific impossibility, another man's treasure," I whispered to Theo.

CHAPTER 10

Theo lived a block over from Main Street, on Ralston Road. There was a white wooden sign staked into the front yard. In bright red letters, it said:

THE BARNES CLINIC
STEPHEN BARNES, DVM

A big red arrow pointed to the left, where the house jutted out past the driveway. In the distance, I could hear faint sounds of a few dogs barking.

Theo walked straight up the path toward the front door. "Can't we go in the other way?" Lucy asked.

"That's my parents' office," Theo said.

"Your parents work together?" I asked, feeling a pang since mine no longer did.

"Yeah."

"They're veterinarians," Lucy supplied.

"Just my dad," Theo said. "My mom runs an animal rescue clinic."

"She rescues animals?" I asked incredulously. "That's the best job I've ever heard of a parent having."

"She doesn't *personally* rescue them," Theo said. "Not all of them at least. People find them, and drop them off. Sometimes the phone rings in the middle of the night because someone found some baby possums on the side of the road."

"Baby possums!" Lucy squealed. "That's so cute!"

"They're not cute at all," Theo said. "They're completely bald and they can't open their eyes."

"Did you get to hold them?"

"No, it was the middle of the night, like I said. I looked it up on the Internet."

"I love animals," I said, following Theo up the porch stairs. "I have a pet rabbit."

"Rabbits have a third eyelid," Theo said. "So they don't blink as often as humans."

"I thought I knew everything about rabbits, but I didn't know that," I said. "Do your parents have rabbits, too?"

"Possibly," Theo said. "I never go over there, since I'm allergic to just about every animal. But I read about them." He held the door open for us. "Come inside. We've wasted enough time already and we have so much work to do."

I called Mom so she'd know where I was. Theo brought down a stack of textbooks from his room, and we sat around the kitchen researching different laws of science, to try and get inspired. The problem was, Lucy and I didn't understand them, and Theo was getting impatient explaining them to us.

"It's not our fault," Lucy said, closing the text in front of her. "This book is like something my brother Oliver would read in college."

"It's an eleventh-grade book," Theo said.

"Same difference."

"Not the same at all," he told her. "At least a two-year difference." He paused and flipped a page. "Do you guys know Newton's first law of motion?" Lucy and I shook our heads, and Theo went on: "An object at rest will remain at rest, and an object in motion will maintain its specific line of motion, unless compelled to change by the application of an external force."

"I don't really understand," I admitted.

"Me, either," Lucy said. "But so what? You think we should invent—sorry, *discover*—a second law of motion?"

"There already *is* a second," Theo told her. "How velocities change when force is applied."

"I guess I'm just not a genius like you," Lucy said.

"I'm not a genius," Theo said. "I work hard, but it's not like I'm in Mensa or anything."

"What's Mensa?"

"It's a genius society," he said. "You need to score in the ninety-eighth percentile or higher on an IQ test to qualify. I'm three points away."

"Three points is pretty close," I told him. "You're still way above average. But I don't think Mr. Dibble expects us to be in Mensa or even close to it to do the assignment. He just wants us to, you know, be curious. So maybe we should think about that instead of the motion laws."

"I tried to tell you about chaos theory before," Theo said. "There's a piece of it called the butterfly effect, which demonstrates that everything matters. Even the small things— even something as seemingly insignificant as a butterfly flapping its wings could change the course of the universe forever. That butterfly could set the wind in motion in such a way that a hurricane is caused on the other side of the world."

I felt myself shiver at the thought. "So if I, like, blow my nose or something, I could cause a tornado?" I asked.

"Technically speaking," Theo said. "But there's no way to know for sure. Unless we discover a way to measure it. Then we could really go global."

"Yeah, sure," Lucy said. "But how?"

"My first thought was to make a terrarium for butterflies, and record their wing flaps, and then monitor the weather in China. But of course there'd be no way of knowing if whatever storms happen over there would've occurred *without* our butterflies."

"Or maybe it'll be because of someone else's butterflies," I said. "On another continent, even."

"I know," Theo said, closing his textbook. "It's not a good idea."

"It *is* a good idea," I told him. "Really. It just may not be possible."

"The problem is, I haven't thought of anything better yet," Theo said.

"Well, you'll just keep thinking," Lucy said. "I will, too." She folded her hands and closed her eyes. "I'm thinking . . . I'm thinking . . ."

I opened my notebook to take notes when and if the ideas came. What was I curious about? At that moment, mostly if I'd get to be an It Girl. If I ate turkey sandwiches every day, would it be enough? What else did I have to do to keep being cool?

"This is hard," Lucy said, her eyes popping open.

"I know," I told her.

"I have a question," she said. "Why'd you join the It Girls?"

I felt my face redden. "You're talking to me?"

"Well, I'm not talking to Theo," she said. "So why did you?"

"How did you know I did?"

"You wrote it on the page."

I looked down. Apparently, without even thinking about it, I'd written an affirmation: *I am an official member of the It Girls Club.*

"I haven't exactly," I said. "I'm in a trial period first, to see if I'm actually It Girls material."

"Hmm," Lucy said. "I don't think you are." I must've looked upset, because she went on quickly. "I'm not saying it to be mean. Honest I'm not. It's just that you're so different from Monroe and the rest of them. You're nice. I don't get why you'd want to be around her. I don't get why everyone does. It's like those moths you see flying into lights for no apparent reason."

"There *is* a reason moths do that," Theo said. "It's called transverse orientation, and it's when insects navigate by flying at a constant angle to a distant light source. Man-made lights confuse them."

"Fine, there's a reason for the moths," Lucy said. "But there's not a reason for *Chloe* to want to be in the It Girls."

"I like them," I said. "We actually have a bunch of things in common."

"Like what?"

"Like . . . Monroe and I both like mushrooms on pizza, and we like the same music and making up dances." I paused. "And I didn't get a chance to be in a club in my old school with my best friend. Now I can be in one here."

"You had a best friend?" Lucy asked.

I nodded. "Her name is Lia," I said. "She's still my best friend. But, I moved away, and she joined a club called the A-Team."

"My brother is my best friend and he just moved to college," Lucy said. "So I understand how you feel. But what about if we make a club with each other, and Theo, too. Like maybe we could have a fashion club. We could all pledge to take more risks with our clothes, and we could even host a fashion show."

"No way," Theo said.

"Okay fine, a different kind of club then. What do you think?"

I shrugged. "The thing is, I'm still hoping to be in the It Girls' club," I said.

The kitchen door banged open. "Hey, nerd!" a girl called.

I saw Theo grit his teeth and tighten his grip on his pencil. "We're working in here," he said.

"Hi, I'm Anabelle," the girl said, paying him no mind. "I'm Theo's sister—you probably couldn't tell since we don't look anything alike."

She had to be kidding, since she and Theo looked almost *completely* alike: same deep red hair, same freckled skin, same eyes. They even each had one eyebrow that was slightly longer than the other.

"I'm nine and I'm in fourth grade," Anabelle continued. "I'm in Mrs. Linvill's class."

"I'm Chloe," I said.

"I'm Lucy," Lucy told her. "I had Mrs. Linvill last year."

"We have to get back to our science project now," Theo said loudly.

"A school project, or a project just for fun?" Anabelle asked.

"A school one," Lucy said.

"Just checking," Anabelle said. "You know what Theo does in his spare time? Reads science textbooks."

"You should read a science textbook," Theo mumbled.

Anabelle went on ignoring him. "Did either of you run track in fourth grade?" she asked Lucy and me.

We shook our heads.

"Theo didn't, either," Anabelle said. "He says he's allergic to running. Which isn't even possible. Plus, our parents were both on the track team when they were young. That's how they met—at a track meet in high school."

"According to Gregor Mendel's genetics research, it's possible I inherited two recessive non-running-genes," Theo said. "It's the same reason that Mr. Dibble's kids have blue eyes, if both he and his wife have brown ones."

Anabelle waved her hand at him. "Yeah, yeah. I gotta go. Mom needs me in the clinic. I'll see you guys later."

"'Bye," Lucy and I called, as Anabelle swung out the backdoor.

"Let's get back to work," Theo said.

"Do you mind if I get some water first?" I asked.

"Go ahead," Theo said. "The cups are in the cabinet above the sink."

I found a pitcher of water in the fridge and poured three glasses. "There you go again!" Lucy exclaimed, as I set a glass down in front of her.

"What?"

"You did something nice."

"I thought you might be thirsty," I said.

"But you do nice things all the time," she said. "Don't you see?"

I looked over at Theo, hoping he'd insist we start talking about the project again. We were dangerously close to the subject of the It Girls being not nice. But he was scribbling in his notebook, flipping a page in his textbook, and scribbling some more.

"What even makes you think of all the nice things you do?" Lucy asked.

"I don't know," I said. "It's easy to do and it makes people happy, and that makes me happy, too."

"It's the serotonin," Theo said, barely looking up. "I just read about it. The more of it your body releases, the happier you feel. And serotonin is released when you act kind, and when someone is kind to you." He pushed his textbook toward us, and flipped back a few pages. "See?"

Lucy and I looked where he was pointing:

Serotonin is a chemical found in the human body. Researchers believe it is responsible for maintaining a person's mood balance. Numerous studies have shown that receiving, giving, or even witnessing acts of kindness increases the production of serotonin, thereby giving the body a mood-boost.

"Does this mean if I do kind things for the It Girls, they'd be more likely to let me into their club for real?" I asked.

"That's a good hypothesis," Theo said.

"Hey!" Lucy said. "We should do this for our project!"

"Oh, no," I said. "I don't mind being kind to the It Girls, but I don't want to do it for our project." Certainly Monroe would think telling the class about how I'd tried to get into the It Girls was the exact opposite of cool. "Besides, it's not science."

"It involves the brain, so that's biology," Theo said. "And human behavior, which is behavioral science."

"You see!" Lucy said.

"But how will we track the sero—how do you say it?" I asked.

"Serotonin," Theo said. "We'd probably need to have access to an MRI machine to know their levels before and after, but if we simply monitor behavior, I bet we can draw some pretty accurate conclusions."

"It doesn't sound like a big enough scientific discovery," I said. "Like the kind that could go global."

"If it turned them nice, it would be good for our whole school," Lucy said. "That's almost just as good. Some kids are even afraid of them."

"I'm not," Theo said.

"I'm not, either," Lucy said. "But some kids are."

I looked between Lucy and Theo, desperately trying to think up reasons why it was a bad idea. "I thought you didn't even want to be in their club."

"I don't," Lucy said. "I bet Theo doesn't, either."

"Not even a Planck length," Theo said.

"Definition, please," Lucy said.

"It's the smallest possible size of anything in the universe," Theo explained. "Around a millionth of a billionth of a billionth of a billionth of a centimeter."

"Still, I wouldn't mind if the It Girls were nice to me and *wanted* me to be in the club," Lucy said. "That would just make things, I don't know, better somehow. You know what I mean?"

"Yeah," I said softly, feeling sad for Lucy, and sad for myself, too. "I do know. But it's called the It *Girls*, which means they'd never be able to invite Theo. And the thing I'm really worried about is if Monroe and the others ever found out we made up a science experiment about them being mean, I bet they'd be really upset."

"It would ruin your chance to get into their club," Lucy said, and I nodded. "It would probably make things worse for all of us," she admitted.

"I have a solution, though," I told her. "We could try to be nice to someone even meaner."

"Who?"

"Mrs. Gallagher," I said. "The question is what will happen if we're kind to her. We already have the background research on the sero—sero—"

"Serotonin," Theo said with an eye roll.

"Right. And our hypothesis is that it'll make her happier, and perhaps even cause her to be kind back."

"How can we possibly be kind to her?" Lucy asked. "As soon as we get within twenty feet, she screams at us to get away. You heard her today. We were just on the sidewalk, which isn't even her private property. It's not like you can get close enough to give her a pencil case."

"She probably wouldn't want a pencil case anyway," I said. "But we could think of other things. Maybe it won't be a *global* scientific discovery, but it'll affect everyone who walks past her house." I turned to Theo. "That's big enough, right?"

"I suppose so," he said.

"Lucy?"

"Can it be our club?" she asked.

"I don't know," I said. "I'm not sure if I'll have time for another club if I get into the It Girls."

"And I definitely can't take time away from my studies for extracurricular activities," Theo added.

"But you have time for this project," Lucy said. "So maybe we start the club just for now. Mr. Dibble said creativity got extra points, and I think a club is creative."

"Me too," I said.

"Theo?" Lucy asked.

"Okay, fine," he said.

"Great! Now all we need is a club name."

"Easy," Theo told her. "The Science Project Club."

Lucy shook her head. "That's about as boring as khaki pants."

"There's nothing wrong with khakis," Theo said.

"I read a book this summer that said wearing khakis tells the world you plan on paying your taxes when you grow up," I said. "Which is a probably a good thing."

"It's definitely a good thing," Theo said. "The alternative is illegal."

"But you can wear colors and still pay your taxes," Lucy said. "Besides, when you look better, you feel better."

"I look fine," Theo said. "I feel fine."

I'd started writing again, without even thinking. Lucy leaned across to look at the page. "What's that?"

"What? Oh, nothing."

"No, that's it!" Lucy said. "Theo, I know you're nearly a genius, but Chloe is an actual one!" She grabbed my notebook and held it up to show him: *The Kindness Club*.

CHAPTER 11

That night Mom brought home takeout from A Slice of Heaven, the pizza place near Regan Halliday's office. "Wow," I told her, as I went for a second slice. "This may be the best pizza I've ever had."

"Even better than the pizza you make with Dad?" she asked.

The bite I'd just taken felt stuck in my throat. I wasn't the one who'd brought Dad into the conversation, but I still felt awkward about it. "We didn't make pizza last weekend," I told her.

"Oh, yeah?" she said. Mom eats pizza with a fork and a knife—don't ask me why—and she'd set her utensils down on the edge of her plate. "Why not?"

"He had some friends over," I said, trying to keep things breezy. "One of them has something called Celia disease."

"I think you mean celiac," Mom said, and I nodded. "Lori in Dad's office has it. It wasn't Lori over last weekend, was it?"

"No," I said. "It was a new friend."

"Who?"

"This girl and her mom," I said. The bite still seemed caught in my throat, and I took a swig of juice to get rid of the feeling. "The girl has it."

"Oh?" Mom said. "What's her name?"

"Sage."

"And her mom's name?"

"Gloria."

"What about her dad?"

"I don't know," I said. "They're divorced." The phantom piece of pizza stuck in my throat felt like it was *growing*.

"What's their last name?"

I cleared my throat and shook my head. "I don't really remember," I said. Even though I did remember: Tofsky. "Anyway, it doesn't matter. Dad thinks she can replace Lia, but I don't even like her."

The corners of Mom's mouth turned up in the tiniest of smiles. "I hear you," she said. I lifted the slice to my mouth to take another bite. A silence settled between Mom and me. The only sounds were her fork and knife gently clinking on her plate.

"I am making new friends, though," I said, after a couple minutes passed. "Here in Braywood, I mean."

"Right," she said. "Did you have fun today at Theo's?"

"I was just doing a science project with him, and this other girl, Lucy. But the friends I was talking about are Monroe, Anjali, and Rachael. You know, the ones who were here on Tuesday?" Mom nodded. "I think Monroe is my best friend of all of them. Not that she's replacing Lia. I've only known Monroe since last Friday, and I've known Lia for half my life. You can't make a new best friend in a week."

"Of course not," Mom said.

"Of course not," I repeated. "May I be excused to call her?"

"Sure. I'll be in the living room, arranging the bookshelves."

"Didn't you do that already?"

"Only twice," Mom said. "I think the third time will be the charm."

I rinsed my plate in the sink and headed upstairs to call Lia. When she answered, she didn't even say hello. She just said, "Hey, Chlo, I'm with Trissa and Bianca in the middle of an A-Team meeting. I'll call you back, okay?"

"Okay," I said. There was a click as I was getting the word out, and I knew she'd hung up without saying good-bye. I called Monroe next. She wasn't home, but at least I got to leave a message, which is more civilized than practically getting hung up on.

I looked over at Captain Carrot. "You know, the funny thing is," I said, "sometimes I think it's easier to be Monroe's friend, because she doesn't know me the way Lia does. It's like . . . it's like when you have new notebooks on the first day of school, and everything is fresh, and you could be anyone."

Cappy hopped from the bottom of his cage to the top.

"I'm doing this science project in school," I told him. "To see if being kind to someone makes them happier. Officially we're experimenting on Lucy's neighbor, because I didn't want to experiment on the It Girls. But unofficially, I'm going to try it out on them, too. I'm going to be as kind as I can to them, so they want me in the club."

Cappy moved back down to the bottom, and started chewing on his toy carrot. "You work on that," I told him. "I'm going to use Mom's laptop to do some work of my own."

Mom's laptop was on the bed in her room. I sat down and pulled it into my lap. I totally meant to look up ways to be kind to Mrs. Gallagher, but I was still thinking about Monroe, and how being kind to her and the It Girls might make them be kind back to me. Maybe that had been the thing that kept me from the A-Team, besides just the letters in my name. I'd never been *unkind* to Lia or Bianca, as far as I could remember. But before today, I hadn't ever thought about how there were kind things to do, to get people to do kind things back. It was too late now, since I didn't go to school with them anymore. But I had a fresh chance with Monroe and the It Girls, to make things work out right.

"*Ways to be kind to new friends*," I typed into the Google search. A bunch of websites popped up, and I scrolled through to see the words of advice: *Say hello and smile*, one link said. Well, of course. I'd always done that. It was basic human interaction. *Ask people about themselves to show you're interested in what they have to say*, said another. I'd done that, too. *Give compliments*, another website recommended. I sat back and thought—had I given any compliments? Yes, I had! When I first met Monroe, I told her I'd liked her bracelet. I was three for three.

Of course, I could always give *more* compliments. As soon as Monroe called back, that's what I'd do. In the meantime, I wanted to come up with more kindnesses—better kindnesses. I typed in another search: "*special acts of kindnesses*." More websites popped up, and I continued to click through.

Pay the toll for the car behind you on the highway. Since neither Monroe nor I could drive, let alone had our own cars, that one wasn't too practical. Okay, next. *Throw someone a surprise birthday party.* Hmm. I didn't know when Monroe's birthday was. I supposed it would be easy enough to find out, but chances were, it wasn't before she and the It Girls would be taking the club vote. *Dedicate a star to someone*. That was certainly kind and special, and probably really expensive.

I clicked another link that promised wise words on kindness, and a quote popped up: "Be kind, for everyone you meet is fighting a hard battle." According to the website, a guy named Plato said it. I didn't know who Plato was, and besides that, Monroe wasn't fighting any battles, so it didn't help anyway. I closed the Internet browser and I hoped the idea for the right kind of kindness would come to me. Mom kept a pad and a pen on her bedside table, and I grabbed them to jot down an affirmation:

When the time comes, I always know the right ways to be kind.

And then I wrote another affirmation, the main one:

I have the best friends in my new school.

CHAPTER 12

Lucy called on Sunday morning. "How was your brother?" I asked. When we'd left Theo's late Friday afternoon, he'd wanted to make a plan for the very next day to start our Kindness Club project, but Lucy said she couldn't, because she and her family would be visiting Oliver at his college on Saturday. Theo had grudgingly agreed our work could wait till Sunday.

"It was totally great until it was time to say good-bye," Lucy told me. "When I have kids, I hope they're twins so they can go to college at the exact same time and not miss each other." There were muffled voices in the background, and Lucy said, "Sorry, Grandma."

"What's wrong?" I asked.

"Oh, nothing," she said. "My grandma just said she'd be too lonely if Ollie and I were away at the same time. But I still wish I were! He goes to the perfect school for me. You pick whatever classes you want to take. Ollie isn't taking any math, and he doesn't have to be anywhere before 10:00 a.m. Plus all the students I met loved what I was wearing."

"What were you wearing?"

"A shirt and jeans," she said. "I stitched the shirt together from an old blanket in Ollie's room, and I belted the jeans with one of his ties. I'm wearing the same thing today, except a different shirt and a different tie. Plus cat ears because his school mascot is a saber-toothed tiger, and that's in the cat family."

"That's really creative," I said.

"Thanks," Lucy said, sounding pleased. "It's garden-appropriate for Mrs. Gallagher's, too—as long as it's okay with you."

"Of course it's okay with me," I said. "You can wear whatever you want."

"I meant if gardening is okay with you," Lucy said. "I called Theo right before I called you, and we thought fixing up Mrs. Gallagher's garden would be a good way to be kind. Unless you have a better idea to try."

I thought about the research I'd done on Friday night, and a bit on Saturday, too. None of the kindnesses I'd found online seemed any better, and of course most of them were things we couldn't do at all. "I think fixing her garden is a really good idea—maybe even the best one," I told Lucy.

"Thanks," she said. "Theo said he'd meet at my house at three o'clock. I'll have my dad stop at a plant store on the way home, so I can pick up some flowers. Any favorite kinds?"

"Yellow flowers mean friendship," I told her, as I pictured Mrs. Gallagher's yard in my head, with all the old sticks and leaves lying around. "But I think we should probably clean things up before we plant anything. We'll need a bunch of garbage bags. I can get some."

"We have plenty of those at home," Lucy said.

"Okay, cool. So we'll go over, and ring her bell, and—"

"I don't think we should ring her bell," Lucy said. "It's better if it's a surprise. Plus, then we won't have to talk to her before everything is all fixed up and she gets happier. You heard how she yells, and that was when we were just on the sidewalk. Ollie rang her doorbell once, when he accidentally kicked a soccer ball into her backyard, and before he even told her why he was there, she said she was going to call the police on him—and on my dad for letting him play unsupervised. He never did get the ball back."

"What if she sees us there and calls the police?"

"We'll just have to be extra *extra* quiet about it. We won't even speak to each other when we're there." There were more muffled sounds, and Lucy said, "Don't worry, Dad. We're not *bothering* Mrs. Gallagher. We're being *kind* to her."

"I hope she thinks so," I said. "Do you—oh, wait, hang on. I'm getting another call." I looked at the caller ID: *REESER, EDWARD*. "Sorry," I told Lucy. "I should probably take this."

"That's okay. See you at my house at three?"

"Yup. See you." I clicked over. "Hello? Monroe?"

"Chloe?"

"It's me." *Quick, think of a compliment to give her.* "Your voice sounds so professional over the phone."

"Gee, thanks," she said. "So, listen, do you want to go the mall today?"

"Oh, yeah, I'd love to."

"Cool. My dad told me he'd take me, but now he has some kind of stupid business meeting."

"On a weekend?"

"Uh-huh. And my mom's rehearsing. So if your mom can drive us—"

"I'm sure she could."

"Great."

"The only thing is, I have somewhere to be at three."

"Where?"

"Lucy's house," I said. "For our science project."

"Ugh," Monroe said. "Will Theo be there, too?"

"Yeah."

"Oh, that's even worse! Poor you!"

"I don't mind," I told her.

"Well, one thing's for sure," she said. "You really need a trip to the mall. We could go now, have lunch, and you'll be back in time."

"I'll ask my mom," I told her. "And I'll call you right back."

A half hour later, Mom and I were in the car on our way to Monroe's house. Actually, *house* was the wrong word. It was a mansion stretching three stories high, and at least three times as wide. The driveway in front was a circle, and Mom pulled around. There were trees cut in fancy twisty shapes on either side of a double-front door.

Monroe ran out and climbed into our car. "I like your house," I told her. "It definitely looks like an actress lives here."

"I know, right," she said. "I'd take you in to meet her, but she can't be disturbed when she's in character. She doesn't even like *me* to disturb her. Because if I call her 'Mom,' or ask her something, then she's pulled right back out to real life."

"I never thought about it that way. But I understand."

"It's cool that you do." Mom had steered out of the drive-way, and Monroe called up to her. "If you need me to tell you the way, let me know. I've gone to the mall about a bazillion times."

"That's all right," Mom said. "Chloe and I have been there before and I've got it."

But when we got to the parking lot, Monroe directed Mom to the right entrance, the one closest to all the best stores. Mom had given me twenty dollars because she thought I needed a few more pairs of underwear—thank goodness we'd had that discussion *before* we'd picked up Monroe. I'd also brought along twenty dollars of my own money from Grandma. Mom said she'd meet us at the same entrance in exactly two hours. Monroe had a cell phone, and Mom made her program her number in.

"You're much more protective than my mom," Monroe told her.

An overprotective mom was clearly not cool, and my cheeks warmed. "She doesn't have to, Mom," I said. "I know your number."

"What if you get separated?" Mom said. She rattled off her number, and Monroe put it in her phone. Then Mom had Monroe send a text, so she'd also have her number, too.

"Thanks for the ride," I said.

"I get the hint," Mom said. "See you in a couple hours."

She drove off, and Monroe led the way to Look Now. I knew from when I'd visited the store with Mom the Friday before school started that it was pretty expensive. But maybe there would be something on sale. Stores always have sale racks in the back.

Monroe, meanwhile, went straight for the mannequin at the front of the store. "Oh. My. God," she exclaimed. "Chloe! Look at these!"

The mannequin was wearing ripped stretchy pants with paint splotches all over them. A saleswoman had rushed over to us. "They're great, aren't they? They just came in yesterday, and they're selling like hotcakes. But we have a few left—in each of your sizes, if you want to try them on."

"Oh, yes!" Monroe said.

"How much are they?" I asked.

"Oh, let's see," the saleswoman asked, fiddling with the price tag in the back of the mannequin's jeans. "Ninety-nine dollars. Plus tax."

I sucked in my breath. "Wow," I said.

"They're hand-painted," the woman explained.

"They're really nice," I said, so as not to hurt her feelings. "I just don't have that much money."

"Sure you do," Monroe said. "I saw. The day we ordered pizza, remember?"

I nodded. "But I only brought twenty dollars of it with me, plus twenty from my mom."

"If you like the way they look, I'll loan you the money for the rest," Monroe said. "Unless you think your mom will be mad."

"No," I said. "My mom says my money is mine to spend. She just won't replace it if I make a bad choice."

"This won't be a bad choice," Monroe said.

"Besides, it doesn't hurt anything to try them on, does it?" the saleswoman said.

"No, it doesn't," I admitted.

"All right, come on then." She ushered us toward the dressing rooms. Monroe picked a few other items off the racks as we went. The saleswoman, whose name turned out to be Judith, brought us the pants in our sizes, and said to let her know if we needed anything. We pulled the curtains to our dressing rooms closed.

"I'm going to count to three and we'll both come out at the same time, okay?" Monroe asked.

"Okay."

"One. Two. Three. Come out!"

I whipped my dressing room curtain open, and stood next to Monroe, in front of the big mirror. Her reflection was a little bit taller than mine, and her pants had a couple more paint splotches on them. But you could tell they were the same, of course. It was like being in a uniform—a really cool uniform.

"Do you love them?" she asked. "I love them."

"I do," I said. "But you saw them first, and I can't get the same thing as you."

"Rachael just said that because she knows I don't like random people to dress the same as me. But I don't mind if you do. You're not random."

"Really?" I asked.

"Of course not. I think I was right about you. I think you're legit It Girls' material."

When she said it. I felt all lit up inside, like I'd swallowed the sun and it was glowing from the inside out. "Thanks," I said.

"How's everything going, girls?" Judith called from behind us.

"Great," Monroe said. "I'm going to take them."

"Me too," I said.

Monroe tried on a few more things, and ended up getting the pants, plus two shirts, a scarf, and a headband. After Judith rang our stuff up, she said we should both wear our clothes out of the store, so we could be twins for the day. Not that we really looked at all like twins, but it was fun to walk through the mall dressed the same. Monroe wouldn't want just anyone to look like her.

We had some time left before Mom was coming to pick us up, and we were both hungry, so we went to the food court for chicken fingers and french fries. There were a couple of people ahead of us in line, and a few behind us. I wondered if they noticed that we matched. If they did, that meant they were also noticing that Monroe Reeser and I were friends. I'd been chosen by Monroe, the way Lia had been by the A-Team. This time I wasn't left out. This time I was a part of something. This time it was me.

Behind us, there was a thump, and then a woman's voice: "Amy Lauren, stop stomping."

"But I'm hungryyyy," replied a little girl. Her hair was in pigtails, but they were messed up, like it was the end of a long, hard day. She drew the last word out like it had four syllables instead of just two.

Her mother's face reddened when she saw me watching. "Sorry," she said. "See, Amy, you need to be patient. You are irritating everyone on this line."

"It's okay," I said. "If you want to, you can go ahead of us."

"Next!" the guy behind the counter said.

"Go on," I told Amy Lauren's mother.

"Thank you, you're a lifesaver," she said, stepping in front of Monroe and me. She placed her order—two chicken sandwiches and an order of fries.

Then it was our turn. "A large order of chicken fingers, large fries, and two small sodas," Monroe said.

The guy behind the counter punched something into the register. "We're just out of fries," he said. "I can ring you up now, and you can come up to the counter in five. Okay?"

"What would happen if I said it's not?" Monroe asked him.

"Uh," the guy stuttered, seeming flustered. "Then I guess you wouldn't get any fries."

It was weird that he was older than us, and he seemed a little scared of us. It made me feel a teeny bit powerful, standing next to Monroe. But then she turned to me. "You shouldn't have let them cut in line," she said.

It was my turn to be flustered. "Sorry . . . it was just . . . I was trying to be nice. That kid looked like she was about to cry. I'm really sorry."

"Psych!" Monroe said. She put her arm around me. "Just kidding, twinsie. It's no big thing."

"So do you want the fries or not?" the guy behind the counter asked.

"Yes," Monroe said. She paid for our meal, since I didn't have any money left. We picked a table near the food stand and waited for our fries to be ready. When they came, they were extra good. Fresh-from-the-fryer warm, with the perfect crispy outside, and soft middle. Even Monroe thought they were worth the wait. "Can we call your mom and see if she'll pick us up a little bit later. There's a new movie I want to see. The one Erin Lindstrom is in. Have you seen it?"

I shook my head. "But I have to meet Lucy at three."

"Tell her something came up."

"I can't," I said. "I promised."

"I know you love being nice to everyone," Monroe said. "But what about being nice to me? I loaned you money for clothes, and I bought you food. And besides, you owe me, since we had to wait so long for the fries."

"I'm sorry about that," I said.

"It'll be a white lie to Lucy," she said. "You can just tell her you have a stomachache or something."

The truth was, right then I sort of did. I wanted to be kind to Lucy. Not just because of the Kindness Club, but also because that's how I was. It was how I liked to be. But I also wanted to do the thing Monroe wanted me to do.

Monroe had her phone out. "I don't even have her number," I said.

"We can Google it. I'm sure she's listed."

"What if she's not home?"

"Just leave a message. Come on. Please? For me—your clothing-twin?"

I hesitated for a second, and then nodded. "Okay."

CHAPTER 13

Lucy was waiting for me outside Ms. Danos's classroom.
"Hey!" she called when she spotted me at the end of the corridor. She was dressed head-to-toe in different floral patterns. And by head-to-toe, I mean literal head, to literal toe:
there was a homemade flower wreath on her head, and little
flower buds stuck in her penny loafers, in the slots where
the pennies were supposed to go. The only thing that wasn't
flowered was the fanny pack belted around her waist. It was
sky blue. "I worried you wouldn't be here today," she said.

"Why?"

"You weren't feeling well, you said."

Unconsciously I placed a hand on my stomach. My
cheeks warmed, and I felt like the lie was written across my
face. Like instead of just ordinary blushing, the words *I lied
to you, Lucy* had popped up in bright red.

"I'm okay now," I said quickly.

"Great!" she said. "Because I have so much to tell you, and Theo said—" At that moment, Anjali came up behind me and put a hand on my shoulder.

"Hey, Chloe," she said. "What are you guys talking about?"

"Our science project," I said.

"How's it going?"

"Fine," I said.

"That's good. How was the movie yesterday?"

"Um," I said, feeling like the worst person in the world for lying to Lucy, feeling like I couldn't even look at her. "It was okay."

"Yeah, that's what Monroe said."

I could feel Lucy looking at me. I looked back, but not at her face. "We should probably go inside," I said to her feet. "We don't want to be late." There were at least five more minutes before the official start of class, but I was too uncomfortable to stand there any longer.

"Yeah, okay." The three of us headed in—Lucy to her seat in front, and Anjali and me to the back, where Monroe was waiting. "Theo wants to have a meeting at lunch today, okay?" Lucy called.

I turned, briefly meeting her eye.

"Come on," Anjali told me.

"So, lunch?" Lucy asked.

"Yeah, sure," I said quickly.

⭐

At lunchtime I walked down to the cafeteria with Monroe and Anjali. We passed by the hot-lunch line—chili that day, fine with me to miss out on—and made our way to the sandwich counter. I put together the usual. Afterward, I walked Monroe and Anjali to the table in the back to say hi to Rachael, and then said good-bye to all three It Girls. Monroe insisted on teaching me a signal, in case I needed to be rescued. The signal was scratching the back of my head with two fingers. I knew it was silly. Lucy and Theo were just kids, and I wouldn't need rescuing from them.

Unless Lucy got mad at me about the movie thing and started yelling, then I *would* want to be rescued. I practiced the signal and headed over.

Lucy patted the seat next to hers. If she was mad about the movie, you couldn't tell, which made me feel a little bit better, and a little bit worse. "Okay, good, you're here," she said. "I have surprises for everyone."

"Surprises, really?" I asked. "Like presents?"

Lucy grinned. "Yup."

"Work first," Theo said. He pulled a notebook out of his backpack. "After the epic experiment failure at Mrs. Gallagher's house, I went back to the drawing board."

"Oh, no," I said. "You didn't tell me it was a failure."

"I didn't get a chance," Lucy said. "Though I was planning to spare you the gory details."

"Something *gory* happened?" I asked, incredulous. I hadn't really believed that Mrs. Gallagher could possibly be a witch, but for a second I reconsidered it.

"There wasn't any gore," Theo said. "There wasn't much of anything. I met Lucy at her house, and we spent about twenty minutes in her grandmother's backyard shed, deciding what supplies to pile into the wheelbarrow and wheel over."

"Mostly rakes and garbage bags," Lucy said.

"And then we spent about twenty *seconds* conducting the experiment," Theo said. "Before we'd even touched a thing, Mrs. Gallagher came running out of her house screaming about trespassing being a criminal offense."

"Oh, no," I said, shuddering. I felt bad for not being there with them, but I also felt relieved that I'd missed being yelled at.

"I don't know how she heard us there," Theo went on. "She wasn't watching by the windows, because we checked. The doors were closed, and we'd barely made a sound. Maybe she eats a lot of bananas."

"I'm sorry, I think I just heard *you* wrong," Lucy said. "Did you just say bananas?"

"Yes, they're rich in potassium," Theo said. "Our internal potassium levels decrease as we age, and that's linked to hearing loss. If Mrs. Gallagher has a special affinity for bananas, it's possible her hearing didn't decrease. Maybe it was even enhanced. But that's a hypothesis for another time. The point is, we didn't get to test things out yesterday."

"You didn't get in trouble with the police or anything, though," I said. "Did you?"

"We ran back to my house too fast," Lucy said. "I accidentally dropped one of my grandmother's gardening gloves. I didn't tell her yet."

"So our hypothesis is disproved already," I said.

"Not at all," Theo told me.

"Huh?" Lucy asked.

"Think about it," he said. "We hypothesized that if we were kind to Mrs. Gallagher, it would make her happy, and even make her kind back. All we proved is that if we walk onto her property with a wheelbarrow, she'll scream at us. We didn't get a chance to be kind to her."

"It's her own fault," Lucy said. "If she'd just stopped yelling and looked around, she could've seen we were going to surprise her with a clean yard."

"Maybe she doesn't like surprises," Theo said. "Not every kindness is right for every person. Like if you baked a cherry pie for Anabelle, it'd definitely make her happy, and maybe she'd even be kind back to you. But if you baked one for me, I wouldn't be able to eat it because I'm allergic."

"You'd probably still be kind and say thank you," Lucy said.

"Of course I would," Theo said. "But Mrs. Gallagher is a harder subject. For that matter, so is my sister. So I conducted some supplemental work." He was leaning forward and talking in a voice that was not unlike the way Mr. Dibble sounded when he was in front of the classroom. He sounded excited.

"What's supplemental?" I asked.

"Extra," Theo said. "Here, I have something to show you."

He pulled out a sheet of paper and slid it toward us.

A Nonexhaustive List of Ways to Be Kind to
Subject #2, Anabelle M. Barnes
By Theodore M. Barnes

1. Smile 0/4
2. Slip her a nice note
3. Give compliments 0/4
4. Ask questions about the other person 0/3
5. Do the dishes (even when it's not your turn) 1/1
6. Draw a picture as a gift 0/1
7. Tell a joke to make her laugh 0/1
8. Read a book out loud
9. Give flowers
10. Give her a hug 0/1 (disaster!)

"I didn't get to try them all," he explained. "But the ones I did try had mixed results."

"Is that what the numbers are?" I asked.

"Yes. Now, you can see, my subhypothesis to our original hypothesis was right. Not everything worked on Anabelle. Smiling and giving compliments were the biggest failures. For example, I told her I liked the shirt she was wearing, and she ran upstairs to change. And each time I smiled at her, she asked me what the heck was wrong with me. They say the definition of insanity is doing the same thing and expecting a different result. But for the sake of research I tried four times."

"Maybe you're smiling the wrong way," Lucy said.

"What are you talking about? I smiled the way I always smile."

"Show me," Lucy said.

"This is ridiculous," Theo said. But then he did force a smile onto his face.

"Hmm," Lucy said. "Did you look at Anabelle like that when you were trying to hug her?"

Theo didn't answer.

"It's just," she went on, "you look like you're in pain. Doesn't he, Chloe?"

"You don't exactly look happy," I admitted.

"I would've been concerned, too, if you looked at me like that," Lucy said. "And if you tried to hug me like that, well."

She shook her head. "I think you should try again. Think of something really special and wonderful, like discovering a trunk full of vintage clothes in the attic, and then smile."

"Special and wonderful are two more things that are subject-specific," Theo said. "But that's not even relevant. Please look at item number five."

We looked.

"My sister despises dish duty," Theo said. "The rule my parents have is that we take turns. Originally, my mom suggested that Anabelle and I do the dishes *together* every night, but Anabelle wouldn't have it. The only thing she hates more than dishes is the idea of doing them with me. So that's why we switch off. On her nights, Anabelle is always trying to talk her way out of it. Luckily, my parents are impervious to her complaints."

I didn't know what impervious meant, but I had a general idea of what Theo was saying.

"Last night it was her turn," he went on. "Anabelle said she was too full, she said she was too tired. She said it was unfair because my dad had made two side dishes, and now there were extra plates to wash. I said, 'I'll take care of it this time.'"

"Was she so happy?" I asked.

"She was so confused," Theo said. "My dad told her not to look a gift horse in the mouth, so she said thanks and ran out of the kitchen before I could change my mind. Later that night, Anabelle came into my room with a bar of chocolate.

She keeps a bunch of them stashed in her room. She's never offered to share before."

"Wow," I said. "So it definitely worked."

"It's too early to draw conclusions," he said.

"What kind of chocolate bar was it?" Lucy asked

"Milk chocolate with caramel. I didn't even eat it. I saved it in case we need it for evidence."

"Evidence?" Lucy said. "What is this? A crime scene?"

"*Scientific* evidence," Theo told her. "So, anyway, when we go back to Mrs. Gall—"

"Excuse me," Lucy said. "Did you say we're going back there?"

"Of course we are."

"But didn't you also say doing the same thing again and expecting a different result is the definition of insanity?" I asked.

"We won't do the exact same thing," Theo said. "We'll find something that works."

"I doubt she'll let us into her house to do *her* dishes," Lucy said. "She'd probably kill us if we tried!"

"Don't worry," Theo said. "We're not going to do anything like it. We're going to write a note."

A nice note was number two on Theo's list. "What will we write?" I asked. "Some kind of compliment?"

"I honestly can't think of any to give her," Lucy said.

"It doesn't matter," Theo said. "Because our note will be our offer to clean her yard up. Instead of taking her by surprise, we'll let her know our intentions—and that those intentions are kind. Lucy can slip it in her mailbox."

"If only she had one," Lucy said. "The houses on my street have slots in the front door."

"Okay, you'll slip it in there," Theo said.

"Oh, no," Lucy said. "I'll just mail it."

"Then we have to wait for it to go all the way to the post office, just to be delivered back to her door, and we don't have that kind of time."

"So you expect me to go *on her property* again."

"Yes," Theo said. "Today, if possible."

Lucy audibly gulped. "Okay."

"I can go with you," I offered.

"Well, that's unexpected," Theo said.

"Unexpected?" I said. I couldn't believe it—that Theo thought it was unexpected that I'd help Lucy. Though I guessed I deserved it. "I'll really go this time. I don't have an It Girls' meeting until tomorrow."

"I wasn't talking about you," Theo said. "I was talking about Anabelle. She just waved to me." He lifted his hand to wave back. "She's never done that before."

I breathed a sigh of relief and turned to wave to Anabelle, too. So did Lucy. "Speaking of things that are unexpected," Lucy said. "I think it's time for the surprises now."

She opened up a flap on her fanny pack and pulled out three squares of felt. "I made us club patches," she said. "You don't know this, Chloe. But I used to make patches all the time."

Lucy handed one to Theo and one to me. They were yellow, and the edges weren't frayed at all. Instead there was blue piping all around, and in the middle green letters stitched in that spelled out *The Kindness Club*. Underneath the letters, Lucy had stitched some shapes, like a fancy kind of underline.

"You sewed these?" I asked incredulous, and Lucy nodded. "I can't even mend a hole. Those letters must've taken all night."

"They practically did," she said.

"And I like the pentagons," I added.

"Hexagons," Theo corrected. "Pentagons have five sides and hexagons have six."

"Okay, hexagons," I said. There were two of them put together, with lines coming out of either side.

"I googled what serotonin looks like," Lucy explained. "It's like having a club logo."

"Wow," I said. "They look really professional. Like something you could buy in a store."

"Thanks," Lucy said. I could tell she was pleased. "You don't have to wear them. I just wanted you to have them."

"I'll wear it," Theo said.

"Even though it's not khaki?" Lucy asked. "What if someone sees you wearing it and thinks you're the kind of person who won't pay his taxes?"

"You can wear colors and still pay your taxes," Theo said.

"Did you hear that, Chloe?" Lucy asked. "I think Theo learned something from us for a change!"

We were fist-bumping each other, à la Mr. Dibble, when Monroe walked up. "Hey, guys," she said. She winked at me, which made me feel like she was there because I'd signaled her. Which I hadn't done. I hadn't raised my hand at all, except to wave to Anabelle.

Oh, right, I'd waved to Anabelle. Monroe probably thought I *had* been signaling her.

"Hey, Chloe," she said. "How's the meeting?"

"It's good," I said.

"It's great," Lucy told her.

Monroe reached in front of me and picked up Lucy's patch. "What's this?" she asked.

"Accessories for our club," Lucy told her.

"Your *club*?"

"Our science project," I told her.

"Lucy made you patches for it?"

"Uh-huh," I said.

"Well," Monroe said. "That's . . . interesting." She dropped my patch back down on the table, the right corner slightly creased from where she'd been pinching it. "So, Chloe, I just came over to tell you that you should come over after school."

"Well, I . . ."

"Rachael and Anjali are coming," Monroe said. "My mom will be home, and she really wants to meet you."

"She does?" I asked.

"Of course."

I looked at Lucy. I looked back at Monroe. I felt pained. "The only thing is, I just told Lucy I'd help her with something for our project after school."

"You can do it another day though, right?" Monroe asked. "You know my mom isn't home every day."

"It's okay if you want to go," Lucy told me.

"That settles it then," Monroe said. "Is your meeting done? If so, you should come back to our table with me—ours is just getting started."

"Almost," I said. "I'll meet you over there."

Monroe walked away, and I gathered up my stuff and said good-bye to Lucy and Theo. "I'm really sorry about this afternoon," I told Lucy.

"It's no problem," Lucy said. "I know you want to be kind to Monroe. I figured that's why you went to the movie when you were sick."

"Yeah," I said. My stomach did a somersault. "That was why."

"Just don't be so kind that you forget all your scientific obligations," Theo said.

"Oh, Theo," Lucy said. "You worry too much. We still have a week left."

"We need Mrs. Gallagher to respond to the note," he reminded her. "And we need to time to rethink things if she doesn't. But it's okay. I'll go with you on my way home."

"Chloe!" Monroe called.

"Go on," Lucy said. "We've got this."

"Thanks, guys."

CHAPTER 14

It turned out Monroe's mother wasn't home that day after all. Bernadette, the housekeeper who lived with Monroe's family, told us that Elle Reeser had taken the train to New York City, to rehearse with friends. "Did she say when she'd be back?" Monroe asked.

Bernadette dragged a damp cloth along the kitchen counter, cleaning a slab of marble that was already sparkling. "Your mother doesn't tell me her plans."

Monroe looked sad, and I put a hand on her arm. "I'm really sorry."

"There's nothing to be sorry for," Monroe said quickly. "This is a big opportunity for her. She's the director's first choice for the part, which means she's about to be a Broadway star. It's what she's always wanted."

"We should all go to New York City and see the show," Anjali said.

"If she gets it," Monroe said.

"You just said she's the director's first choice," Rachael reminded her.

"Yeah, she is."

"Hey, do you have any of those wafer cookies we ate last time?" Anjali asked.

"Bernadette?" Monroe said, in a voice that made it sound like we'd been waiting on the wafer cookies for at least a year.

"I'll make a tray," Bernadette said.

"We'll be out back," Monroe told her. She turned to the three of us. "Let's go."

"I need to call my mom first," I said.

"Yeah, sure," Monroe said. She nodded toward Bernadette, who handed me a phone.

I dialed Mom's number, and let her know I was perfectly safe and at Monroe's house. When we hung up, I headed to the backyard, where the other girls were sitting on lounge chairs. I sat on a cushy chair next to Rachael, and looked across the backyard, which was as big and well kept as a golf course.

"Can you believe the Spanish homework?" Rachael asked. "Two sections of the workbook."

"Totally excessive," Monroe said.

"I can help you if you want," I said. "I started Spanish in my old school, so I'm a bit ahead of things."

"Is that what Rivera wanted to talk to you about after class?" Anjali asked.

I nodded. "She said she was going to give me some other assignments, to work on while the rest of the class caught up."

"Teacher's pet," Monroe said.

My cheeks warmed and I stared off at the vastness of the backyard, for a few seconds not saying anything.

"What's that?" I asked, breaking the silence and pointing at a brown square in the distance.

"It's a dance floor," Monroe said. "My mom had it installed years ago. She used to be a dancer, and she says you never know when you're going to want to dance in the backyard."

"My mom has never ever danced in the backyard in her life," Rachael said. "Your mom is so cool."

"Yeah," Monroe said softly. She paused for a second, and I wondered if she really thought so. Then she added, "Hey, Chloe, let me see that patch again."

I didn't know what had made Monroe think of Lucy's patch right then. But I really wished she hadn't. "It's in my backpack in the kitchen," I told her, hoping she wouldn't tell me to go back in and get it.

Bernadette came outside with a tray of wafer cookies, plus cheese and crackers, and four glasses of seltzer over ice.

"Thanks," I said.

"Oh, hey, Bernadette, get Chloe's backpack for her. It's in the kitchen, and it's the—what color is it?"

"Blue," I said. "But—"

"This will be great. You guys can see Lucy's handiwork. There's a weird squiggle at the bottom, like she was trying to make a cool design, but failed completely."

Bernadette was already halfway back to the screen door. "Wait," I called. "You don't need to."

"She doesn't mind," Monroe said.

"But I have a better idea," I said. "Let's practice our dance on the dance floor. It's a much better space than my living room, and we don't have to worry about the couch getting in the way."

"Bernadette, turn on the speakers for us, will you?"

"You got it," Bernadette said.

Phew. Saved by a backyard dance floor.

CHAPTER 15

I missed the It Girls' meeting on Tuesday, because I had an orthodontist appointment. Mom picked me up straight after school and took me to Dr. Beach. Then we ran a few errands, and stopped at a diner for dinner. When we got home, there was a voice mail from Monroe. I went up to my room to call her back, and she answered on the first ring. "Hey, I was hoping it would be you," she said.

"Really?"

"Yeah, we were talking about you at the meeting today, and we had an idea. But first I need to be sure about something. You want to be in our club, and not one with Lucy and Theo. Right?"

"Absolutely. I even told them," I said.

"What did you say *exactly*?"

I'd taken Captain Carrot out of his cage. Now I was lying on my bed, with him on my stomach. I balanced the phone between my shoulder and my ear and put both hands on his back. "I said I didn't think I'd have time to be in a club with them," I told her. "I said if I got in, I'd have a lot of stuff to do with you guys."

"Okay. That's good. I think Lucy may have the wrong idea about you. I talked it over with Anjali and Rachael, and we think there's only one thing to do—you need to give Lucy back the patch."

"Give back the patch?" I asked.

"You can do it tomorrow," she said. "Sit with her and Theo at lunch. And when you're done, you can give me the signal—the same one we had before."

"But—" I started.

"I've got to go," she said. "But tomorrow. Lunch. You know the signal."

I hung up the phone and rubbed Cappy's soft back. I could feel the beat of his heart under my fingers. When I first got Cappy, I worried something was wrong with him, because his heartbeat was so fast. But it turned out that's normal for rabbits. Right then, it seemed like my own heart was beating at the same pace, way faster than a normal human's.

Mom knocked on my doorframe and came into the room. "Hey, sweetie," she said. "Do me a favor—when you're with your dad tomorrow, can you make sure to get a check from him?"

"A check for what?"

"The money he owes me for your school clothes," she said. "Plus his half of your orthodontist consultation."

"I thought Dr. Beach wasn't charging us," I said.

"What gave you that idea?"

"Because he knows Dad."

"Dad gives him referrals sometimes, so he's giving us a small discount, but nothing is ever free."

"Oh," I said. "Well, can't you ask Dad yourself when you drop me off?"

"You know your dad doesn't come out to the car," she said.

"So you can call him," I told her. "Or you can come outside when he drops me off after dinner."

"Give me a break, Chloe, won't you?" Mom said. "It'll take you a few seconds to ask for the check, and a few seconds for him to write it out. He's the one who passed on the crooked teeth anyway. He had braces for five years."

"Five *years*?"

"Your teeth aren't nearly as bad as his," Mom assured me. She motioned for me to move my legs and sat down beside me. "You've seen the pictures of your dad as a kid." I nodded, and Mom went on. "There was this story Grandma Barb once told me. Your dad was so afraid of the dentist that on one visit, he jumped out the window. It was only the first floor. But still—a pretty drastic reaction, don't you think?"

"Yeah," I agreed.

"I always liked that story," Mom said.

"You liked that he jumped out a window?" I asked. Things between my parents were bad, but I didn't know they were so bad that she wanted him out a window.

"I liked that he grew up to be the thing that scared him," Mom said. "He once told me it was because he wanted to give dentists a good name. No kids out his office window."

"That'd be really dangerous since his office is on the third floor," I said.

"You bet it would," Mom said. She smiled a closed-mouth smile, and suddenly her pressed-together lips got thinner, and she looked slightly pained. For a few seconds a silence fell between us. I wondered if she was thinking about that office on the third floor. There was cream-colored carpeting in the reception area, a beige couch, and a mahogany coffee table and side tables. The receptionist's name was Grace, and then there were the dental hygienists, Lori and Annmarie, who worked on the patients with Dad. They'd been Mom's friends. And now they weren't anymore.

"I'll ask Dad for the check," I told her.

"Thanks, sweetheart," she said. "You have a great smile already. It'll be even better."

When she left, I turned back toward my rabbit, sitting on my belly. We locked eyes and stared at each other, like one of those staring contests Lia and I used to have when we were little, to see who could go the longest without blinking. I knew Cappy had a slight advantage, because of his third eyelid. I tried my hardest not to blink, but my eyes started to ache. Blink, blink. "I guess I lose," I told him.

CHAPTER 16

Lucy hadn't heard anything back from Mrs. Gallagher, she told us at lunch the next day. She and Theo were both eating cheeseburgers and tater tots. I had my usual, a turkey sandwich. Even though I wasn't sitting with the It Girls, I knew they were watching, and I wanted to do the right thing. "But I did some supplemental work of my own, in the meantime," she said.

Theo chewed and swallowed. "Details?" he asked.

"I'm getting to them," Lucy told him. "I knew my grandmother had a really busy day. Monday is one of the days she volunteers at the food pantry. Plus my dad's assistant at the bowling alley—"

"Your dad has a bowling alley?" I asked.

"Yup, Tanaka Lanes," Lucy said proudly. "Make a left on Main Street, and a right on Sheridan, and you're there!"

"Wow, everyone's parents have the best jobs," I said.

"You can come anytime you want," Lucy said.

"Thanks."

"You guys always seem to get off topic," Theo said. "Can we get back to your supplemental work?"

"By the way, Theo," Lucy said. "You're invited to Tanaka Lanes anytime, too. But as I was saying, my grandma had a busy day, because she volunteered and filled in at the bowling alley. The manager cut back on his hours, so that's why. She left a note that she'd be home a little bit late. I saw a pile of laundry in the basket in the hall, and I decided to help her out. I'd never used the washing machine before, but I thought to myself, *Lucy, how hard can this be?* And the answer was, *Not too hard.* I lugged the basket over to the machine, and threw the clothes in. The cap on the soap stuff doubles as a measuring cup, so it was easy to figure out how much to pour in. I wasn't exactly sure what buttons to press, but somehow I got it working. It was really fun. I never thought laundry would be so fun, but it was."

"Serotonin at work," Theo said.

"Your grandmother must've been happy," I said.

"Well, that's the thing," Lucy said. "When I pulled everything out to put in the dryer, it had changed colors. I thought maybe it looked a little, like, bluish, because it was all wet, and sometimes water is blue."

"No, it's not," Theo said. "It's just that the other colors are absorbed more strongly by water than blue is. Same with the sky."

"Anyhoo," Lucy said. "I put it in the dryer, and when it came out, the white things were still a bit blue. Turns out you're not supposed to mix colors like that."

"Oh, no!" I said.

"My dad was really mad when he saw—like *really* mad. I tried to explain I'd just been trying to do a kind thing and I'd made a mistake, but he said I shouldn't have helped if I didn't know what I was doing. He said it'd cost a lot of money to replace things I'd ruined. My grandmother was great about it, though. She told him to go start dinner. I'd already set the table, and at least I hadn't messed that up, and he calmed down and said he knew I had the right intentions. Then my grandmother showed me how to separate clothes, and use bleach for the white things. She managed to get all the blue out, so our stuff looks normal again. Plus she seemed to appreciate what I'd tried to do. I think it still counts, don't you?"

"Definitely," I said.

"Yes, I think so," Theo said. "Because the act was perceived as kind. Which is our problem with Mrs. Gallagher."

"More like *Mrs. Gallagher's* problem with *us*," Lucy said.

"Po-tay-to, po-tah-to," Theo said. "Either way, we put all our eggs in one basket, and we need to diversify."

"I don't know why you're talking about eggs and baskets."

"It's a metaphor," Theo said. "What I mean is, we left her a note and that's the only thing we did."

"Plus the supplemental stuff," Lucy reminded him. "We'll have plenty of things to write up in our report."

"Are we supposed to write a report?" I asked. "Or is it just a presentation to the class?"

"Mr. Dibble didn't specify," Theo said. "Sometimes I wonder about his teaching skills."

"Be kind," Lucy chided.

"I'm not saying anything unkind," Theo said. "I'm stating a fact: I wonder."

It was like the summer reading. Those details hadn't been specified, either. But I doubted that Mr. Dibble had been trying to trick us into work. Not that I knew him well, but that didn't seem to be his style.

"Let's ask him after class," I said.

"All right," Theo agreed. "Now back to Mrs. Gallagher. It occurs to me that when we left the letter we didn't take into account all the things that could go wrong. She could've thrown it away accidentally. Or maybe she read it, but she didn't think cleaning her yard was a kind thing to do."

"How could she not?" Lucy asked.

"I guess it's possible she likes things messy," I said.

"Precisely," Theo said. "So this is what I think we should do. I think we should leave her another note."

"But she could throw that one away, too," I said.

"No, she won't because we'll put it in a care package."

"What kind of care package?" Lucy asked.

"We'll have to brainstorm on that," Theo said. "And then we'll put everything in a box or basket or something, and put a note on top, offering to clean her yard, if she wants. We can do it this afternoon."

"There's only one problem," Lucy said. "Wednesday is my piano lesson day. I won't be home till later."

"And I have dinner at my dad's tonight," I added. "But I can think of things and e-mail you."

"All right," Theo said. "And then we'll put the care package together tomorrow after school."

"Works for me," Lucy told him.

I turned around. Monroe was staring at me. She caught my eye and nodded. I turned around again. "I have an It Girls' meeting, and I missed it yesterday, so I can't miss another." I paused. "Hey, Lucy. Can I give you something?"

"Oh my goodness, you have a present for me?" Lucy squealed.

"Hold on," Theo said. "We need to figure this out."

"It's already figured out," Lucy said. "We'll each brainstorm care package ideas for Mrs. Gallagher, and Chloe can bring whatever she wants to add to school tomorrow, and then you and I will drop it off. Okay?"

"Okay," Theo said.

"Okay," I said.

"Okay," Lucy said. "Now, what do you have for me?"

"Um," I said. I pulled my backpack onto my lap, and unzipped the small pocket. The patch was right there.

I knew Monroe was watching, but she couldn't see exactly what I was doing, since the backpack was in my lap, and my back was to her. I pulled out the sunshine pocket mirror from Lia's sister's party, and handed it to Lucy. "Here," I said. "Because it's your favorite color."

"Oh my goodness!" Lucy said. "You're so kind! This should count as supplemental work because it's definitely giving me more serotonin. Thanks, Chloe!"

I shifted my body closer to her, blocking Monroe's vision even more. "You're welcome," I said. Then I raised my hand, and scratched my head, and gave the signal.

At the end of science class, Lucy, Theo, and I went to talk to Mr. Dibble. "What can I do for you?" he asked.

"We have a question about our project," Theo said. "Do we give an oral report, or hand in something written, or both?"

"What?" Mr. Dibble asked, looking confused for a moment. "Oh, right. You know, the truth is, I didn't have anything specific in mind. So whatever works best for the three of you, works for me."

"If we do both, will we get extra credit?" Theo asked.

"Hmm," Mr. Dibble said. "I suppose that would be all right. Sure thing."

"Thanks," we told him.

He fist-bumped each of us. "You're a terrific trio," he said.

"We prefer to call ourselves the Kindness Club," Lucy told him.

"I like that," Mr. Dibble said. "I'm expecting great things."

Monroe was standing outside the classroom when we walked out. "Hey, Chloe," she said. "I waited for you."

"You didn't have to do that. I can't even really hang out today, because I have work to do, and then I have to go to my dad's."

"I know," she said. "I'll walk you home."

"But my house isn't on the way to your house," I said.

"I'll walk with you anyway," she said. "I just have to go to the bathroom first."

"Oh, sure, of course," I told her.

I said good-bye to Lucy and Theo, and followed Monroe down the corridor. She pushed open the door marked "girls." It was a small bathroom, only two stalls, and they were both empty. But Monroe didn't go in either of them. At first I didn't think anything of it, because she stood in front of the mirror and fixed her hair, while I went into the one on the left. "I heard what Lucy said to Dibble," she called to me through the stall door.

I could tell by her voice that it was something she disapproved of, and scrunched up my eyes, trying to remember what Lucy had said, what Monroe could possibly be talking about.

She said the words the very same instant that they popped into my brain: "The Kindness Club," she said. "Even though you told *me* that you told her you didn't want to be in it."

"I *did* tell her," I said. "Like I told you before—I told her that I didn't think I'd have time to be in it, once I got into the It Girls." I'd finished in the bathroom, flushed, and I pushed open the stall door. "It's just for this project. Just until Monday. I promise."

I watched Monroe's face to see what she was thinking, but it was hard to tell. She certainly didn't look happy with me. But she didn't necessarily look that mad, either. She stepped aside so I could wash my hands.

"I like your hair like that," I said, watching her in the mirror, hoping my compliment would work some kind of magic—or at least some kind of science.

"Thanks," she said. "I guess you did give the patch back, since I saw you give the signal at lunch today."

I pulled a paper towel from the dispenser and dried my hands.

"And your project *is* done on Monday," she said.

"That's right."

"But trust me, Chloe, you don't want to be seen doing things with them any more than you have to. I'm just looking out for you."

"I know you are."

"Good." She gave herself one last glance in the mirror. "I think it's safe to go now."

"Don't you have to go to the bathroom?" I asked.

"Oh, no," she said. "I just said that so Lucy and Theo would get a head start walking home and wouldn't try to walk with us."

We headed out to Braywood School Road. At the crosswalk, Monroe made a left with me, toward my house, instead of going straight toward hers. She pulled a disposable water bottle out of her bag and took a swig. "Want some?" she asked. I shook my head and she put the cap back on. "Have you noticed what close friends Anjali and Rachael are?"

"Sure," I said. "The three of you are really tight."

"We are," she agreed. "But the two of them, well, the thing is, I've always been the head of the It Girls, so I know everyone likes me and looks up to me. But when there were four of us, it was better. Rachael and Anjali were a pair, and I was a pair with Haley. The other two were still my friends—they're like tied for second-best-friend in my life. But Haley was my best friend. It was totally unfair when she moved away."

"I understand," I told her. "When we moved this summer, I had to leave my best friend. Her name is Lia, and we've always had each other, ever since the first day of kindergarten. She dropped her cream cheese bagel on the ground and I offered her half of my peanut butter and jelly sandwich, and that was it, we were best friends."

"Haley and I were best friends from the first day of kindergarten, too. Our teacher, Mrs. Tilly, kept mixing our names up. I think because we were the only two kids in the class who had a french braid."

"Is that why the It Girls wear french braids on the first day of school?"

"Yup," Monroe said. "It became our tradition, and when we started the club, Anjali and Rachael wore them, too. I figured it would always be like that, but then Haley's mom got a new job last spring, in New York. It was for a lot of money. I told my dad to offer Mrs. Booker a job for even more money. My dad owns his own company, so he can do things like that. But he said no. Even when I begged. He said kids shouldn't meddle in adult decisions. I don't think that's fair, since kids have to live with the decisions the adults are making."

"That's exactly how I felt about it when my parents said they were getting divorced," I told her. "They said they were selling my house, and I'd be switching schools. They didn't ask me what I thought about it."

"Of course they didn't," she said, and she shook her head. "Parents."

"I think I've found the best friends in my new school, though," I said. It was the closest I'd come to saying my affirmation out loud; well, except to Captain Carrot. "I always try to find the bright side of things, and that seems like a pretty bright side, don't you think?"

Monroe didn't answer right away, and I was afraid I'd said the wrong thing. It was hard, waiting to see if I'd get to be an official It Girl. I always felt like I was in the middle of a test. But then Monroe linked her arm through mine, and I felt relieved, as if my whole body had just exhaled. "Let's skip," she told me.

We skipped down the next two blocks, until we had to stop for a red light. Monroe chucked her water bottle into the garbage can on the corner. "Wait," I said. "There was still water left, right?"

"Oh, sorry," she said. "I thought you said you didn't want any." She plucked it off the top of the garbage. "I don't think it touched anything gross."

I unscrewed the cap, walked over to the tree on the corner, and poured the leftover water around its roots.

"It was for the tree?"

"I'm not thirsty," I said. "But trees always are, right?"

"OMG, Chloe. Only you," Monroe said, but she had a smile on her face, and I was pretty sure it was a compliment. I smiled back and swung my backpack around to unzip the front pocket. "Now what are you doing?"

"I'm putting the bottle away to recycle it at home."

"Only you," Monroe said again. "Here, I'll unzip it for you." I could feel her fiddling with the zipper, and sticking a hand in the front pocket. "What's this?"

"What?" I said.

She pulled away from me, Lucy's patch in her hand.

"Monroe, I can explain," I said. "Lucy had just said something really nice, and well, you know . . ." My voice trailed off. "I wanted to be kind."

"God, you're so obsessed with that," Monroe said. "The whiny kid at the food court, and the water for the trees, and Lucy's patch. But what about how you lied to me? Doesn't keeping this when you said you wouldn't count as being unkind?"

"I guess I just didn't know what was so bad about keeping a patch," I told her.

"I'll tell you what's so bad," she said, shaking her head. "There are people who do what they say they're going to do, and then there are people who say they'll do something but they're just lying."

"I didn't want to upset you," I told her.

She shook her head. "Here, take your stupid patch. I've got to go."

CHAPTER 18

When I got to Dad's, the first thing he told me was that Gloria had a great idea for a special dinner for us. "Us, meaning you and me?" I asked.

"Of course you and me. And Gloria and Sage, too." He took my backpack from my shoulder. "Why the glum face, Chloe?"

"I thought I'd get to spend a little time with you tonight," I told him.

"You will, bear," he said. "I'll be there, too. Besides Gloria's the one who had the idea for dinner. It's gluten-free, so Sage can eat it. It's the right thing to do to include them, don't you think?"

"Yes," I admitted.

"I knew you'd want to do the right thing," he said, though I'd said nothing of the sort. "You're my girl. No one is as important to me as you are."

"Really?"

"Of course. That's why I want you to spend time with Gloria and Sage. They're important to me too."

I felt tears prick my eyes, but I blinked them back fast. "I have homework to do," I said.

"I thought the deal was you do homework before you see me on Wednesdays."

"I didn't finish yet," I told him. "I have a big science project, and I might have to work all through dinner."

"Do you need my help?" Dad asked.

"No, thank you," I said.

I headed to my room and sat down at my desk, thinking about what to do for Mrs. Gallagher's care package. I wasn't in the mood to be kind to anyone, especially since being kind didn't seem to be working out the way I wanted it to. I tried to think back to when that had changed, and I was pretty sure it was when I told Dad to get yellow roses for Gloria. Or maybe it was before that, when I gave Lucy the pencil case.

None of it would've ever happened if Mom and Dad hadn't split up.

I was still at my desk when the doorbell rang. According to the clock in my room, it was 6:14. I wondered how long it would take for Dad to come get me to see if I was ready to make dinner with them, and I watched the numbers change. 6:15. 6:16. 6:17. There was the sound of laughter from down the hall, but no footsteps to my room, no knock on the door. Not until after seven o'clock.

By the time the knock finally came, I'd given up staring at the clock and watching the minutes tick by.

Knock, knock.

"Yeah?" I said.

It was Sage—not Dad—who pushed open my door. She didn't step into my room. She just hung in the doorway, picking at her nails. "Your dad said to tell you dinner is ready."

"I'll be there in a minute," I said.

"Okay."

She headed back out to the hall. I closed the school book in my lap, but I waited a couple extra minutes before I headed out, just to see if Dad himself would come to check on me, which, of course, he didn't.

When I got to the dining room, the three of them were sitting around the table. Sage was next to Dad again, in my seat. But worst of all, in the center of the table was a platter of sushi.

"Chloe!" Gloria exclaimed, spotting me standing by the counter. "Come, check out the fruits of our labor!"

I wouldn't have minded some fruit right then.

I glared pointedly at Dad. "Gloria's great idea for dinner was sushi?" I asked. I knew I was supposed to be polite, especially when we had guests, but I couldn't help myself.

"Homemade sushi!" Dad said. "We rolled the fish up in rice and seaweed using bamboo mats."

"But I hate fish," I said.

"I'm sorry," Gloria said. Her eyes slid toward Dad's. "I heard you liked fish."

"She does like fish," Dad replied. He turned to me. "You *do* like fish."

"I think you have me confused with your other daughter," I said.

"Very funny," Dad said. "I've seen you eat fish at least a dozen times."

"You've seen me eat *shellfish*—shrimp and lobster and things like that."

"And swordfish," he pressed.

"But it was cooked. I'd never put raw fish in my mouth."

"Never say never," Dad said.

"No, thank you."

"Chlo—"

"Jimmy, don't push her," Gloria said.

"Fine," Dad said. "You can make yourself a grilled cheese if you prefer."

I went into the kitchen and pulled out the grilled cheese—making supplies. Usually I made my grilled cheeses with cheddar, but all Dad had on hand were the crumbly kinds of goat and blue cheese that you put on a salad. When it was done, I brought my plate over to the table. Dad and the Tofskys were still talking about the sushi they'd made, trying to decide what was more delicious—the raw salmon or the raw tuna. Dad said salmon, but Gloria and Sage were stuck on tuna. I was stuck on the fact that both choices were raw.

Dad picked up a piece of tuna, and Gloria leaned over and chomped it off Dad's chopsticks before he could himself. "Hey!" he said.

"I think the tuna should go to someone who truly appreciates it."

Dad looked over at me. "I wish you'd try this," he said. "At least it would end in a tie."

"Or she could like what *we* like," Gloria said.

"No, no, no," he said. "I know Chloe's taste buds. Come on, taste a piece." He picked up a piece of salmon, stood, and held his chopsticks out across the table toward me.

I shook my head. "You don't know me as well as you think you do," I said.

"I'll eat it," Sage told him.

"I thought you didn't like the salmon," Dad said.

"I just like the tuna more," Sage said. "But if you're giving that piece away, I'll take it."

"Sounds to me like you may be turning Team Salmon," Dad said. He moved the piece of sushi toward Sage. "That's my girl."

That's my girl. I couldn't believe he said that to her. "Give it to me," I said.

"Really?" Dad asked.

I reached out, pinched the salmon roll between my fingers, and popped the thing in my mouth. I chewed and chewed and chewed, but it seemed to be growing bigger. It took me like a year to swallow. They were all staring at me, waiting. "Well?" Dad asked.

"Disgusting," I said. I reached for my water and gulped the whole thing down.

"I guess the tuna victory stands," Gloria said.

I took a bite of my grilled cheese, which had turned cold by that point, and tasted like feet. Worse than that. It tasted like feet that'd been sweating in gym socks all day. I'd already put my taste buds through so much, and I couldn't help but gag into my napkin. Once again all eyes were on me. "You okay, Chloe?" Dad asked. Gloria thumped me on my back, which sent chills down my spine.

"The grilled cheese is awful," I said, tears pricking behind my eyelids.

"You didn't make it the way you like?" Dad asked.

"You didn't have the right cheese!" I told him. "All I wanted for dinner tonight was pizza. I thought that's what you meant when you said a special dinner, because we didn't get to have it on our regular night. But instead it's like I'm being food-punished. We haven't had anything I've wanted because . . . because . . ." My eyes slid toward Sage. "Well, you know."

"All right, that's enough."

"I'm sorry she's allergic or intolerant or whatever, but why do I have to suffer so much?"

"I don't expect you to suffer. I expect you to be kind."

"I am being kind! I'm being kind all over the place! It never works out!"

Dad's voice was low and grave. "This is not kindness, Chloe. I'm disappointed in you."

"Do you feel a song coming on?" I asked him sarcastically. I honestly couldn't remember ever speaking to my dad like that before. He didn't answer. I stole the quickest glance at Sage, in *my* seat. Her head lowered toward her plate, like she was the one who had something to be really sad about.

"Maybe we should go," Gloria said.

But Dad put a hand on her arm. "No," he said.

"I'm going to my room."

"Yes," Dad said. "I think that would be best. You and I will talk about this privately, later."

But Dad and I didn't talk about it later. We didn't really talk at all for the rest of the night, except when he came to my room to tell me it was time to drive back to Mom's house. I sat in the backseat instead of the front, just to put a little more distance between us. He pulled up in front of our white house on Parrott. The house he'd never been inside.

My hand on the door handle, ready to go. "Chloe," Dad started.

I saw a shadow by the window, and I knew it was Mom, waiting for me, waiting for Dad to drive away. "I need a check for your half of my braces," I said.

"Oh, right. I have one in my wallet." He shifted in his seat and reached into his back pocket. When he handed it over, I stuffed it into my backpack and got out of the car without saying good-bye.

So there was the bright side of my dad being disappointed in me: that check was the one easy thing to ask him for.

CHAPTER 19

I got to Ms. Danos's classroom just as the bell rang, so I didn't get to talk to Monroe until we were walking down the hall toward the cafeteria. "Hey," I said, catching up to her and Anjali. "Can we talk for a sec?"

"I'm on my way to lunch right now," she said.

"Could I walk with you, then?"

"It's a free country," Monroe said.

She was walking quickly. Anjali was, too. I picked up my pace to stay beside them. "Okay, well, I just wanted to say that I'm really sorry about yesterday—really and truly sorry."

"It's fine," she said, barely glancing my way.

"Really?"

"Really."

"Oh, thank goodness," I said. I'd been saying affirmations in my head all night—one for Monroe, and one for my dad.

I have the best, most forgiving friends at my new school.

Dad forgives me and we make cookies together.

"So, is the meeting at your house today?" I asked.

Monroe spun around. "You think you're going?"

"Well, I thought that . . ."

"You thought all you had to do was say you're sorry. Tell me this—are you sorry that you lied and said you'd do something and then you didn't, or are you just sorry you got caught?"

"If I had to do it over again, I would've done it differently," I told her.

"You didn't answer the question," Anjali said.

We'd reached the cafeteria, and other kids were pushing past us. Monroe pulled on Anjali's arm. "Come on," she said. "I'm going to try the salad bar today. Shake things up a bit."

"It's just that it's complicated," I said.

"Nothing complicated about it," Monroe said. "I know what kind of person you are now. We took a vote on it last night and the decision was unanimous: you are not It Girls' material after all."

"I'm sorry," I said. "Isn't there a way I can make it up to you?"

"I'm really hungry," Anjali said.

"Me too," Monroe said. "Let's go."

CHAPTER 20

I ended up eating with Lucy and Theo, and Lucy tried to distract me so I wouldn't feel so bad, but it didn't help. Nothing did. It's not that I wished I'd been mean to Lucy; except, actually, a part of me did. A part of me wished that I'd given her back the patch instead of lying to Monroe about it, so I could be sitting with the It Girls at lunch, and be welcome at their Thursday after-school meeting.

Instead, Theo, Lucy, and I went to Lucy's house, to put together the care package for Mrs. Gallagher. I brought the paper flowers I'd made late the night before, like the ones Lia and I had made for our mothers last Mother's Day. Except these I'd dipped in blue paint, not pink or yellow. Blue meant something that was impossible, and honestly that's how being kind felt to me right then. Like no matter how hard I tried, I wouldn't get it right.

Lucy exclaimed over them anyway: "These are *amazing*, Chloe!" She herself had made an infinity scarf, cut from one of Oliver's old blankets that she'd been repurposing for different fashion things. Theo had done chores for Anabelle in exchange for some of the best items in her candy stash. Lucy's grandmother gave us a basket to use, and we wrote up a note to Mrs. Gallagher, explaining that we were trying to be kind, and offering to help her in her garden over the weekend.

"I just have one problem," I said. "I leave for my dad's tomorrow, so I can't do weekend garden work with you. But I can type up our written report, so it's fair."

"I started it already," Theo said.

"Of course you did," Lucy told him.

"Send me what you have and I'll add to it," I offered.

"How can you add to it if you won't be here this weekend to see what happens?" Theo asked.

"I'll add it for her," Lucy said.

"It's fine," Theo said. "I can do it."

"I feel bad," I said. "I need to do *something*. I can . . ." I paused, thinking. "I can be the one to drop the basket on her porch."

"I thought we'd do it all together," Lucy said.

"Three people's footsteps are louder than one person's," I said.

"She's right," Theo said. He picked up the basket and handed it to me. "It's go time."

Lucy and Theo walked me out to the Tanakas' front porch. "Good luck," Lucy said. "We'll wait right here and be the lookouts. If we see her approaching the window, we'll give you a signal."

"A signal?" I asked, thinking of Monroe, and the patches, and the signal I'd given her.

"Chloe's not going to be looking at us," Theo said. "The only signal we can give is a shout. Besides, if there's trouble, chances are she'll see it first."

Lucy shuddered. "It's okay," I told her. "I'm not scared." And I wasn't. I knew Mrs. Gallagher wasn't a witch. She was just an old woman with a mean streak, and she couldn't do anything to hurt me. The people with that kind of power were hanging out at Monroe's house right then. Maybe they were even talking about how glad they were that I wasn't there, too.

If possible, Mrs. Gallagher's house looked even more run-down than the last time I'd seen it. I stepped over branches crisscrossing the walkway, up to her porch. There were old newspapers lying around. I pushed a couple aside and put the basket down.

That's when the door creaked open.

Of course there was no such thing as witches. Of course there wasn't.

But if there *were*—they'd look a lot like Mrs. Gallagher did up close, of that I was sure. She had a face of someone who had lived a hundred years, a hunched back, and gnarled fingers, one of which was pointing right at me.

"You!" she said. "What are you doing here? Does your mother know where you are?"

"She's . . . she's at work," I stammered.

"And your father?"

"He is, too," I said.

Mrs. Gallagher shook her head in disgust.

"I'm sorry," I said. "I was just . . . I was just leaving—"

"That's right!" she snapped. "Leave! Off my property!"

She didn't have to tell me twice. I scrambled down the steps, hopped over the branches on the walkway, and was back on Lucy's porch before I'd even taken my next breath. Lucy had the door open, and we all ran inside. She closed it behind us, and turned the lock for good measure.

Mrs. Gallagher wasn't a witch. She couldn't hurt me. I knew all that. But my heart was beating like Captain Carrot's, or maybe even faster, and it took a few seconds to catch my breath. Meanwhile, Theo walked over to the window in the den, which had a view of Mrs. Gallagher's porch. "You guys have to see this," he said.

"Did she pick up the basket?" Lucy asked.

"She kicked it," he said.

"What?" I asked.

"She kicked it," he repeated. "Then she went back inside. Look."

Lucy and I came up behind him to see the basket we'd carefully prepared was lying on its side, my flowers on the ground beside it.

"I can't believe she did that," Lucy said. "I mean, I guess I *can* believe it, because she's the meanest person I've ever known—meaner even than some girls who go to school with us, who shall remain nameless."

Her eyes shifted to me. My body already felt flushed from my close encounter with Mrs. Gallagher, and my cheeks warmed even more.

"It's possible that Mrs. Gallagher's body simply doesn't manufacture serotonin, in which case she wouldn't have experienced any joy from our kindness," Theo said. "Or maybe, given her age, it takes longer for it to kick in. We should watch the house for a bit, to see if anything happens."

"You think she'll come out again and turn the basket back over?" Lucy asked.

"Possibly," Theo said. "Is it all right if I pull a chair up and watch for a little while?"

"Sure," Lucy said. "Put three chairs up. I'll get us some popcorn. It'll be just like watching a movie."

"Cool," Theo said.

"Actually, guys," I said. "I'm not really feeling that great. Is it okay if I just head home?"

"Oh, poor Chloe," Lucy said, putting an arm around me. "Mrs. Gallagher scarred you for life."

"No, that's not it," I said.

"Is it about what happened with Monroe?" she asked, and I nodded miserably. "Well, you still have us," Lucy went on. "And I hereby declare this to be an emergency meeting of the Kindness Club. Theo, quick, we need to do a bunch of kind things for Chloe to cheer her up!"

"Extra popcorn?" he suggested.

"No, thanks," I said. "I'm sorry, you guys. I don't think I should be in this club anymore. I mean, I'll be in it until Monday when our project is done. But this isn't the right club for me, either."

"What are you talking about?" Lucy asked. *"Of course* it is. You're the kindest person I know."

"I'm not as kind as you think I am," I told her. "The day when I was at the mall with Monroe, and I was supposed to meet you guys, I wasn't really . . ."

"What?" Lucy asked.

"I lie about things," I said, my eyes flashing hot with tears behind them. "I lied to you when I said I didn't feel well that day. You weren't mad at me, but you should've been. I didn't do it to be kind to Monroe. I did it to be kind to me. And in the end, it didn't work out anyway."

"Oh."

"I have to go now," I said.

On the walk home, I thought about all the people who used to think I was kind, but didn't anymore. Lucy, Monroe, Sage. Actually, Sage never thought I was kind in the first place, but my dad sure did. He used to be proud of me for being a certain type of person. Everything was different since I'd moved to Braywood. *I* was different. Tears pricked behind my eyes again as I walked slowly home. Affirmations for Dad and the It Girls swirled in my head:

> *I have the best, most forgiving friends at my new school.*
> *Dad forgives me and we make cookies together.*

And suddenly, I knew what to do.

I picked up my pace, running the rest of the way and up the stairs to my room. There was thirty-two dollars left in the envelope in my desk drawer. I pocketed it and ran back outside. I was out of breath by the time I made it to the grocery store on Main Street. Mom had been driving each week to the bigger store, a couple towns over. But I didn't have a car, or much time, and this was my only shot. Luckily everything I needed was there. I had just two dollars and forty-one cents left when I walked out with a paper bag full of ingredients for Dad's famous chocolate chip cookies.

Back home, I preheated the oven, which I'd never done on my own before. But I'd baked cookies with Dad so many times, and I knew the steps by heart. Measure each ingredient, mix them up, spoon the batter into baby fist-sized balls, and place them on a cookie sheet. A half hour later, I pulled the second tray of perfectly golden-brown cookies out of the oven. I barely let them cool before wrapping them in tinfoil and setting off again, this time to Monroe's house.

While the cookies had been baking, I'd prepared a speech in my head about how I hoped the cookies would prove how sorry I was. I raised my hand and rang the doorbell: *ding DONG ding.* It stopped, and there wasn't a sound from the other side of the door. Seconds ticked by. Then minutes. I wondered if Monroe and the It Girls had spied me coming up the walkway through the peephole, and were pretending not to be home. My palms had started to sweat and the package of cookies felt slippery in my hands. I seriously considered turning around and heading home myself. But I knew I had nothing left to lose. I raised my hand and rang the bell again.

Ding DONG ding. For a couple seconds, more silence. Then there was a shout from inside: "Yeah, I heard you. I'm coming." A moment later, the door swung open. Monroe stood on the other side of the threshold. Her eyes were as cold as a lake iced over, and they narrowed in on me in a death stare. I thought of an expression Lia used to say: *If looks could kill . . .* In that moment, if they could, I'd be a goner.

"What are you doing here?" Monroe asked.

"I . . . uh . . . ," I stammered. My carefully prepared words had flown out of my head. "I brought cookies."

"You brought *cookies*?" she asked, like it was the most absurd thing she'd ever heard.

"Yeah," I said, as I felt my cheeks flush with fresh embarrassment.

"Why?" she asked.

"Because, uh, everyone likes cookies. I knew you guys were meeting and I thought that—"

"You thought you could get me to forget how you lied," Monroe supplied. When she put it that way, it did seem pretty absurd. "But you can't. I won't. The other girls won't, either. And besides that, we canceled today's meeting. You should offer your little treats to your other club."

"I'm not in that club anymore," I said. "Listen, I know I messed things up with you. I messed things up with everyone. But I still want to . . . I still want to make things right with you."

Monroe made a move like she was about to close the door. "Please just—" I started.

"MONROE BETH REESER!" a voice boomed from behind her. A man strode into the foyer. He was tall, at least twice my height, in a navy suit, white shirt, and a loosened red tie. When I pitched my head back to look up at him, I saw he had the same dark brown hair as Monroe (though the sides of his hair were brushed through with gray), and the same eyes, which he had focused on her in the same death stare she'd been giving me.

"Dad?" Monroe said in a voice so meek it was hard to believe it was actually coming from her.

Mr. Reeser waved a piece of paper at his daughter. I could tell it had once been folded up into a tiny square, because there were creases crisscrossing it. "Bernadette found this in your jeans pocket when she was doing laundry," he said. "I guess you need to find better hiding places."

Monroe dropped her head.

"Didn't I ask you about this?" he said, glancing at the solid gold watch on his wrist. "About ten minutes ago? Didn't I?" It seemed like another rhetorical question. But when Monroe didn't reply, Mr. Reeser repeated, his voice even louder: "DIDN'T I?"

"You did," Monroe admitted, softly.

"Lying to me is unacceptable, Monroe," he said. "UNACCEPTABLE!" My body shook with the volume of his voice. Monroe's hair was pulled back in a ponytail and

I could see the tips of her ears were bright as beets. Her cheeks matched, and her eyes were round and shiny.

"I think I should go," I said.

"That's a good idea," Mr. Reeser said. "And feel free to spread the word to the rest of Monroe's friends that she's not allowed to invite anyone else over until further notice."

"I didn't invite *her* over," Monroe said. "She's not even my friend."

"Is she not your friend in the same way you didn't get your Spanish test back yet—your *failing* Spanish test?"

"It was a quiz," Monroe said.

"Quiz, test, it makes no difference."

"It *does* make a difference," Monroe insisted. "A quiz counts for way less than a test does."

"School is your job, Monroe. I expect you to come back with grades that reflect how you take your job seriously. Just like I take *my* job seriously." Mr. Reeser lifted a meaty hand, gesturing to the columns on the porch that stretched above us, and looked straight at me. "You can tell I take my job seriously, can't you?"

"Yes?" I said, saying the word like I meant it as a question.

"You hear that, Monroe?" Mr. Reeser asked. "Your friend said yes. I work hard, and that affords my family certain rewards. Which means you get to live in this house, and go on nice vacations, and buy all the clothes you want. I suspect you wouldn't like it one bit if I decided to take things at the office a little bit less seriously. Now would you?"

Monroe gave an almost imperceptible shake of her head.

"You're just like your mother," he continued. "She works when she feels like it. She's a wife and a mother when she feels like it. It's very disappointing. Now here you are, picking and choosing when to honor your obligations. I'm afraid that you're well on your way to turning into another disappointment."

That word got to me: "disappointment." I was a disappointment to my dad, and she was a disappointment to hers. Of all things to have in common.

"Excuse me, Mr. Reeser?" I said. "It wasn't Monroe's fault."

I could feel Monroe's icy eyes on me. I knew she was worried that I was about to make everything worse.

"What wasn't her fault?"

"The Spanish quiz," I said. "You see, I just moved here this summer, and it's only my second week of school. Mr. Dibble asked her to show me around."

"He's the principal," Monroe told him.

Mr. Reeser nodded. "Go on."

"Mr. Dibble made her show me around, and that took up a lot of time. But we started Spanish at my old school, so

I came here to help her, as a thank-you." I glanced over at Monroe. She was looking at her dad, not me, and I turned back to him, too. "And also to give her these cookies as a thank-you," I added. "I won't take up so much of her time again. I swear."

Mr. Reeser stared at me without speaking for what felt like a year. Then he pressed Monroe's quiz into my hand. "You have your work cut out for you," he said, and he turned to walk back inside.

Monroe and I stood on the porch, regarding each other awkwardly. "I'll really leave now," I said. "I promise that I won't ever bother you again. I guess that's the kindest thing I can do for you."

"No!" she said quickly, and I looked up at her. Her eyes had lost their icy glare, and there was a pleading look to them. "You heard him. You have to teach me Spanish." She paused. "Please."

I nodded. Monroe sat down, right there on the porch, and I sat beside her. I still had her red-marked Spanish quiz in my hands, and I put it on the stone step between us. "So I think you're having trouble with your conjugations," I started.

Monroe gave me a look like, *duh*. I went on explaining how conjugating verbs works. "You know, if Rivera explained things to me like that, I wouldn't have failed," Monroe said. She shook her head. "And if Bernadette didn't suck up to my father so much, it wouldn't have mattered in the first place. I bet she couldn't wait till he got home from his business trip, so she could show him the test."

"Quiz," I reminded her.

"Whatever." She nodded at the package in my hands. "So what kind of cookies are those anyway?"

"Chocolate chip."

"Can I have one?"

"Of course. I brought them for you." She took the cookies from me and peeled back the tinfoil. When she took a bite, she closed her eyes in culinary satisfaction. "That's delicious," she said.

"Thanks," I said.

"Haley used to make these cookies she called 'kitchen sink cookies,' where she threw everything you could imagine into the batter—chocolate chips, butterscotch, marshmallows, you name it, she added it. But I've always liked plain cookies best."

"Me too," I said.

"Even though I like toppings on my pizza."

"Mushrooms," I said.

"Exactly."

"Aren't you going to have a cookie?" she asked.

I took one and ate it slowly. My stomach still felt a bit jumpy. I knew it didn't mean we were friends again, just because I'd helped her with Spanish verbs. But something had shifted between us. There was no doubt about that.

Monroe chewed and swallowed, and reached for a second cookie. "Thanks for these," she said. "And thanks for, you know, helping me. Not just for actually explaining it to me, but for what you said to my dad. That was cool. So—thank you."

"You're welcome."

She laughed to herself and shook her head. "You just can't help trying to be nice to people, can you?"

"Is that a bad thing?"

"It is when you lie."

"I just lied to your dad," I reminded her.

"It wasn't really a lie. You already promised to help me with Spanish." I nodded. "Besides, it was for a good cause," she added.

"I honestly thought it was a good cause when I lied to you about the patch," I said. "I was trying to be kind to everyone."

"I get that," she said. "It's just that people who lie to me—it really drives me crazy. My mom, well. The truth is, my dad was right about what he said."

"He wasn't right about everything," I told her. "You're not like that. You're really loyal to your friends. And what I did—I'm really sorry. I shouldn't have lied to you."

"So if you had to do it again, would you give Lucy back the patch?"

"No," I admitted. "Because I wouldn't want to hurt her, either. She's never done anything to hurt me."

"She's so weird, though."

I didn't know how to respond to that, because the truth was we were all pretty weird, in our own ways. And Lucy wearing weird clothes seemed like just about the best kind of weird a person could be. Besides, now that I'd gotten to know Lucy, her clothes didn't even seem all that weird to me anymore.

"I thought it was a white lie," I said. "Like how you said I should tell Lucy I had a stomachache when really we went to the movies." I saw Monroe's mouth twist slightly, remembering. "That's why I pretended I'd given back the patch," I continued. "But I should've told you the truth. And except for the almost lie I just told your dad, I'm going to tell the truth from now on. That's why I brought the cookies. I thought if you liked them, maybe you'd let me explain."

"And give you a second chance at being an It Girl?"

"Yeah, maybe," I said. "But even if it was too late, I still wanted to make up with you."

"Would you help me with Spanish again? Like before the next quiz, so I'll get a grade my dad finds acceptable?"

"Of course," I told her.

"Okay, here's the deal," Monroe said. "I'll give you a second chance. But not a third one. And you've got to agree to some things, too."

"I still don't want to give Lucy the patch back. She worked hard on it. To give it back would be really unkind."

"I understand."

"You do?"

"Sort of," Monroe said. "Enough so that you don't have to give it back. But you do have to promise not to ever stitch it onto your backpack. You wouldn't want to have that patch permanently on your bag anyway. Right?"

"Right," I said.

"So it's settled. I'll tell the other girls that you're in the club."

"You mean I'm not on trial anymore?" I asked. "I'm really in?"

"We're supposed to vote," Monroe said. "But I'm the president, so in the end what I say goes. I'll call them tonight, and you can sit with us tomorrow. Okay?"

"Yeah, okay," I said. "I mean, great—that's really great."

We said good-bye, and I started home. I walked slowly, taking the long way through the park, since I had so much to think about. Like how I was relieved that Monroe had stopped being mad, and how I was happy to be an It Girl. But also that I was a little bit sad. It was weird to be sad about not being in the Kindness Club.

What had changed? I wasn't quite sure. But I almost wished we hadn't started a club together, so we didn't have to end it.

But at least we'd probably get a good grade out of it, which was the point, and a pretty good bright side.

I turned the corner on to Parrott Drive. There was my house, second one from the end of the block. And there, in the driveway, were two police cars. I broke into a run.

CHAPTER 21

Something must've been really, horribly wrong. I took off down the block faster than I'd ever run in my life. When I banged through the front door, my breath was caught in my throat and my heart was pounding in my chest. "Mom!" I screamed. "MOM!"

An unfamiliar man's voice came from the living room: "She's here."

Mom ran out. She said my name, "Chloe," so soft like it was part of her breath. She pulled me toward her and clutched me tight. I had to push her away a little, because I couldn't really breathe.

"Give her some air," another voice said, a woman's this time. When Mom released me, there were two officers standing in the front hall with us. Mom was crying. She wiped her nose with the back of her hand, something I'd never seen her do. She used to hate when I did that, when I was little. She always said, "That's what tissues are for, sweetheart."

"Where have you been?" Mom asked. Her eyes were glowing with anger, and when I glanced over at the police officers, they were looking at me sternly, too. I realized when the officer had said "she's here," he hadn't been talking to me about Mom; he'd been talking to Mom about me.

There was a beep of a walkie-talkie, and the woman officer lifted it to her mouth and said, "The subject is home. We're coming back in."

"Oh my God, Mom," I said. "I forgot to call you."

"You sure did." Her voice had taken on a low tone I'd never heard before. "I was in a meeting with Regan, and I called Mrs. Wallace as soon as I realized you hadn't called. She came over here, and didn't find you. So I called school. I called your friends. Lucy said you'd gone home upset."

"Did you call Monroe's? I was there for a while."

"There was no answer at Monroe's house, or on her cell. I raced home."

"You left work early?"

"What do you expect me to do when you're missing?" Mom asked rhetorically. "The kitchen was a mess."

"I was going to clean it up."

"I worried someone had burst in here and taken you. I've just been here, waiting and imagining every awful thing that could possibly have happened to you." Her voice cracked, and that brought tears back to my own eyes. I wiped my own nose with my hand.

"Mom, I'm sorry. I'm so sorry," I said. I turned to the officers. "I'm sorry," I whispered to them.

"I trust you won't forget to call your mother again," the man said.

"I won't," I said, sniffling. "Not ever. I promise."

"Call your father," Mom told me. "He's been worried sick."

"Is he home?"

She shook her head. "Call his cell."

"I guess he's not that worried then," I said, more to myself than to Mom.

"What?" she asked.

"I just mean, if he's on his cell then he's out somewhere, probably with Gloria—I mean, probably with his friends."

"He's been driving all over town looking for you," Mom said. "Go to your room and call him. I'll be up when . . . I'll be up when I can breathe again."

I went upstairs and dialed Dad's number. He answered with an anxious, "Any word?"

"Dad," I said. "It's me."

There was a choking sound, and silence for a couple seconds. Then Dad said, "Chloe. My God. Where have you been?"

"I was at my friend Monroe's," I said. "I swear I'll never go anywhere without calling you or Mom ever again."

"You bet you won't," Dad said.

"Did you have to leave work, too?"

"I left as soon as your mom called," he said. "I have two patients who have to wait another day, in pain, for their root canals."

"When you see them tomorrow will you tell them I said sorry?"

"I will," Dad said. "And when I see *you* tomorrow, we'll discuss your punishment."

"I didn't mean to do it," I said.

"I know," he told me.

The line clicked. "Jim?" Mom said.

"Hi, Emily," Dad said.

"Chloe, say good-bye to your father and do your homework," Mom told me.

"'Bye, Dad," I said.

I hung up and pulled my math and English notebooks out of my backpack and sat at my desk. But knowing you scared your parents so much that they cried doesn't exactly put you in the mood to do any work. After a while I stood up and lifted Captain Carrot out of his cage. I sat on the floor and held him close as I imagined Mom imagining all the awful things that could have happened. My tears fell on his soft head.

Eventually, Mom knocked on the door, and peeked her head in. "All right," she said. "I think I'm ready to talk now."

"I'm sorry," I told her again. "It will never happen again."

"I know it won't. But just to make sure, Dad and I are grounding you."

I'd never been grounded before. But I'd never done anything to deserve it. Mom sat on the floor next to me. Our backs were against my bed. I set Captain Carrot on the floor. We watched him hop around the carpet for a few minutes, and then Mom shifted and put her arm around me. I leaned my head against her shoulder. If I were any smaller, I probably would've climbed into her lap. But being next to her, this close, was almost as good. I was still crying a little bit, but it was a good kind of cry, the kind where you're relieved that everything is going to be all right.

Mom had her other hand on my hand, and she squeezed. "Are you okay?" I asked her.

"I am now," she said, squeezing my hand again. "Those couple of hours of not knowing where you were—those were probably the hardest parenting hours I've ever had."

"Harder than when I split my chin ice-skating and needed nine stitches?"

"I hated seeing you in pain," Mom said. "But I knew a bad cut wouldn't kill you."

"Harder than when you and Dad told me about the split?"

"That was a hard day," she said. "This was worse."

"And when we moved away from Dorr Road?"

"We always had each other, you and me," she said.

"And Captain Carrot, too."

"Of course, Captain Carrot," she said, and she reached out a hand to pat his back. "I know the last few months haven't been easy for you, Chloe. You've been so good about it."

"Except today," I said.

"Today was not your finest hour," Mom agreed. "And it just wasn't like you. Did something happen?"

I shook my head. But then I said, "Actually, yeah, a bunch of things did."

"Do you want to tell me about it?"

I hadn't wanted to, but now suddenly I did. I told her about the Kindness Club patches, and Monroe and the It Girls, and how it was impossible to be kind to everyone, but I'd made cookies because I'd wanted to try. "I didn't tell you everything when it was happening, because I didn't want to make you upset," I told her. "I wanted to be perfect."

"Oh, Chloe," Mom said. "I'm sorry you felt like you couldn't talk to me. You can. You always can. You don't need to be perfect. But you have to let me know what's going on."

"It's not like you could change anything," I said.

"That's true," Mom said. "But sometimes it feels better to talk things out, don't you think?"

"It feels better to talk things out with you," I said. "I'm so lucky you're my mom. I'm sorry about today."

"So you've said. A few times."

"Well, I'm sorry a million more times. I'm sorry that you worried so much, and I'm sorry you had to talk to Dad. You guys can go back to not speaking again."

"We were never not speaking."

"Sure you were."

"Chloe, you're our child. We're your parents together. We'll always be on speaking terms."

"But you made me ask Dad for the check."

Mom gave a hard nod. "I shouldn't have done that."

"It's okay. I knew you didn't want to," I said. "And I want to be kind to you."

Mom let go of my hand to rub out an invisible stain on her slacks. "Is that why Dad thought you were angry at him? Because you had to ask him for the check?"

"Dad said I was angry with him?"

"He said you'd gotten upset at dinner last night, and you hadn't spoken to him on the ride home. He worried that had something to do with you making cookies and disappearing."

"Dad was *here*? Inside the house?"

"Chloe, you were missing. Of course he was here. The only reason he wasn't here when you got home was because he was looking for you. I would've been out looking, too. But the police felt it was important for one of us to stay home."

"Oh."

"So why were you angry at your dad?"

"He was angry at me."

"I got that much from him," Mom said. "Are you going to tell me why?"

Captain Carrot was nibbling the sole of my shoe, and I pulled him back into my lap. "Dad has a new girlfriend," I mumbled into the rabbit's fur.

"What?"

I lifted my head. "He has a girlfriend," I repeated.

"Gloria," Mom said.

"Yes," I said. "How did you know?"

"I've known your dad a long time," she said. "It wasn't hard to figure out."

"But did you figure out that Gloria's daughter Sage has a dad that lives a few thousand miles away, and that *my* dad has kind of stepped in and he just loves her."

"I didn't know that."

"It's true," I said. "But I hate her. Gloria, too."

"I've never heard you say you hated anyone," Mom said.

"There are people I hate," I told her. "Like, I hate Hitler, and I hate the guy who was the dictator in Russia that Uncle Russell once told me about."

"Stalin?" Mom asked.

"Yeah, him."

"I've never met Gloria or Sage," Mom said. "So I'm not speaking from personal experience here. But I do

suspect it's probably not fair to lump them in with Hitler
or Stalin."

"Okay, so they never killed anyone," I said. "At least not
that I know of. It's just . . ."

"What?"

"It seems dumb now," I said. "But Gloria sits in your old
seat. Well, not really your old seat because it's a new table.
But it's exactly where you would sit. And Sage sits in my
seat, and she's always bragging about everything she can do,
like her perfect dives, and being in the school play. So I was
mean to her about how she can't eat bread."

"Sage is the one with celiac?" Mom asked.

I nodded. "It's not that I actually care so much about
what we eat at Dad's," I said. "But sometimes I think he for-
gets what it was like when we were all together." I paused,
and took a long breath. "Sometimes I think I'm forgetting it
myself."

"Oh, sweetheart," Mom said. "I understand exactly
what you're saying. Yesterday I noticed the lightbulb in
the upstairs hall was out, and I climbed up on a chair to
replace it, and it didn't occur to me until afterward that I
hadn't changed a lightbulb since before I married your dad,
because he was the tall one."

"That's what I mean," I said. "He reached the high
things, and cooked dinner, and you knew everyone's
schedule, and made sure I cleaned my room. Now it's all
mixed up."

"I think it's a sign that we're growing," Mom said. "I felt good about changing that lightbulb."

"I still wish Dad were here to do it," I said.

"I know it's harder now, Chloe. Maybe it'll always feel a little bit that way. But what you were saying before, about forgetting. I think that means it's starting to be okay. I think that means that this new life is feeling normal. And I want that for you. I want it for me too."

"I do, too," I said.

"I'm glad we're talking about this," Mom said. "I think you should talk to Dad, too."

I shook my head. "I don't know. It all just feels . . . I don't know. Do you think he'd still be married to you if you liked the way he sang?"

"No one likes the way your father sings," Mom said.

"But what about if you cooked with him, like Gloria does?"

"No, I don't," Mom said. "Honestly I don't. The thing about being married—it's much bigger than what anyone makes for dinner. It's more than I could ever describe. Being married to your dad, well, it was like taking a really big trip—parts were magical, and parts were tough, but I wouldn't change it. Especially since I came home with the best souvenir."

"What was that?" I asked.

She pulled her arm back from behind me and twisted around to face me, and put her arms on my shoulders. "You," Mom said. "You."

I smiled. "Kind of like a bright side?"

"Kind of like all the stars in the sky put together," she told me. "I'll never make you ask for the check again. Not that your dad minds paying for these things. He doesn't, and I don't, either. It's a pleasure for us to share expenses for you, because we love you so much and there's no one else in the world we'd rather spend our money on. But it's not your job to be kind to me that way, and I'll be better about what I ask of you from now on, okay?"

"Okay."

"And I hope you feel better about telling me what you're thinking."

"I do," I said.

"Good. Now. Is there anything else you want to talk about?"

"Do you know if there are cookies that people with celiac can eat?"

"There sure are," Mom said. "I can get a recipe from Lori in Dad's office."

"You're still in touch with her?"

"Occasionally."

"Could you get the recipe now, then?" I asked. "And can we go to the supermarket? I know I'm grounded, but couldn't this be an exception?"

"Well," Mom started.

"And can I borrow money?" I added. "I used it up on the ingredients for the cookies I made today."

"You spent all your money from Grandma on cookie ingredients? What did you put in them—gold?"

"The pants I bought with Monroe were pretty expensive," I admitted. "Ninety-nine dollars. Plus tax."

"Oh, Chloe," Mom said. "You're ten years old. You know I don't want to tell you what to do with your own money, but you certainly don't need hundred-dollar pants. I'm forty-two, and *I* don't need pants that expensive."

"I know," I said. "But it was important to Monroe. She wanted us to be pants twins."

"You shouldn't have to pay your way into friendships, sweetheart."

"I don't have to pay for anything else," I told her. "I'm in the It Girls now. And if you loan me the money for the gluten-free ingredients, I'll pay you back, I promise. You don't have to give me an allowance until I do. Please?"

Mom glanced at the books on my desk. "Did you finish your homework?"

"Not exactly," I said. "I've been, you know, pretty distracted."

"Do your homework," Mom told me. "I'll loan you money, and we can go on the way to Dad's house tomorrow night."

CHAPTER 22

On Friday, I was back in the It Girls, and it was like nothing had ever happened. We headed to the cafeteria, skipping the hot-lunch line for the sandwich bar. "Hang on," I told Monroe. "I just need to tell Lucy something about our project. I'll be right back."

Before she could tell me not to, I'd jogged over to where Lucy was. She'd gotten her food already and was by the water dispenser. I looked at her tray with a bit of envy: it was macaroni and cheese day.

"Hi," I said.

"Hi."

"Did anything happen with Mrs. Gallagher?"

"No," Lucy said. "Theo and I watched for an hour before he had to go home, and this morning when I left for school, the basket was still there, kicked over. But it's okay.

Mr. Dibble said he cared more about the process than the results. Plus we have our supplemental work, and Theo started making some graphs last night."

"That's good," I said. "I can help."

"I don't think he needs any help," Lucy said.

"Oh. Okay."

"Chloe, come on," Monroe called.

"One sec," I said.

"I guess you made up with her," Lucy said. "With all of them."

"I did."

"I'm happy for you," Lucy said. "You got the friends you wanted."

My affirmation automatically popped up in my head: *I have the best friends in my new school.*

"Chloe!" Monroe called again.

"I'm coming," I said. "Well, 'bye Lucy."

" 'Bye."

Mom dropped me at Dad's that evening, after taking me to the supermarket first, just like she'd promised. When I walked into the building, he put his arms around me. "I know you know that what you said in front of Sage was wrong," he said, once he'd released me.

"I'm really sorry," I said "And I promise I won't do it again."

"I'm glad to hear that. We'll call the Tofskys a little later so you can apologize to Sage yourself."

Dad took my duffel bag from me, and I carried my backpack. "I really hate apologizing out loud," I said. "It's so embarrassing."

"I think what's embarrassing is doing the thing you need to apologize for to begin with."

I was walking ahead of Dad, so I got to the third-floor landing first, and I held the door open for him. When we got to Dad's front door, he unlocked it, and held the door open for me.

"Speaking of apologies," he said. "I owe you one, too. And I owe you an explanation. The first thing you need to know is I love spending time with you. There's no one I'd rather be with. When you're not here, I talk about you all the time."

"Really?"

"Of course. Sage is a great kid, don't get me wrong. But you'll always be my number one."

"Even if she jumps off every high board and gets the lead in every school play?"

"Even then," Dad said. "The only thing you have to do to impress me is be you."

"I'm not a disappointment to you anymore?"

"You're never a disappointment," Dad said.

"You said I was," I reminded him. "When I said those things to Sage."

Dad shook his head. "I was disappointed in your behavior," he told me. "But you yourself are never a disappointment. Do you understand what I'm saying?"

"Sort of," I said. "Actually, not really."

"There's a difference between doing something bad and being bad. We're all capable of doing bad things. But you, my sweet Chloe-Bear, you are not a bad person. You are my pride and joy. You are thoughtful and generous and kind. The proudest thing in my life is that I get to be your dad. Sometimes you do disappointing things, the same way I know I sometimes do things that disappoint you. We're only human after all. But I think we can both do better, don't you?"

"Yeah," I told him. "I think we can."

"I miss you when you're at your mom's, and I'm so excited when you're here that I want to show you off. But that wasn't being fair to you, because I wasn't thinking about the fact that you probably don't want to be shown off all the time. And I'm sorry about that. This weekend, it'll be just us."

"Did you already tell Gloria and Sage that?"

"I did," Dad said.

"I *do* want some time for just us," I told him. "But, actually, I was hoping we could see them, too. Mom called Lori and got a recipe for gluten-free cookies, and we picked up all the ingredients."

"Where are they?"

"In my duffel," I told him.

"I wondered why it was so heavy. It felt like there were a couple bricks in there!"

I smiled. "It's called xanthan gum," I told him. "Will you help me make them, Daddy-o?"

"I would love to," he said.

But first there was business to take care of. Dad called over to the Tofskys', and talked to Gloria first: "Hi . . . yes, Chloe's here. . . . We're fine, and you guys? . . . That's good. . . . That's great. . . . Well, Chloe has something she'd like to say to Sage. Is she around?"

Gloria must've said yes, because Dad handed the phone to me. My palms were super sweaty and I was making a slippery mess of the phone, just waiting for Sage to come on the line. But once she did, the apology itself didn't take very long. I said, "I said some things I didn't mean the other day, and I wanted to say I'm sorry."

And Sage said, "That's okay."

I said, "It's not really okay. But that's why I'm apologizing."

She said, "I accept your apology."

And that was that. Before we hung up, I asked her if she and Gloria wanted to come over for dinner the next night. Dad and I had discussed that I should get to be the one doing the inviting. Sage said she'd talk to her mom and call us back. I was a little worried that the answer would be no, and that would mean she didn't really accept my apology. But Sage called back to say they'd be there.

They came over just before seven o'clock on Saturday. Dad and I had done all the cooking already ourselves, and we had a taco station set up with all the fixings. Corn tortillas are completely safe to eat if you have celiac disease, and Sage had two of them. She had sat down in her usual seat, which used to be my usual seat. But it was okay. I was getting used to my new seat, and our new company. Sage seemed nice and not at all braggy. Maybe I'd just been oversensitive to it before, thinking Sage was a new-and-improved daughter who was replacing me. Or maybe Dad was right and Sage had just been doing it to try and get me to like her. And now that I did like her, she could relax and just be herself.

Afterward, Dad cleared all our plates and piled them by the sink, and I brought out the cookies. I'd hidden them in the pantry so Sage wouldn't see them until dessert. I'd wanted them to be a surprise, and it was totally worth it. Sage ate a cookie, and then went for a second. "Do you like them?" I asked.

"Are you kidding?" Sage asked. "I just ate two cookies without even breathing. They're the best things I've ever tasted."

"Hold on," Dad said. "Better than anything *I've* ever made for you?"

"Well . . . ," Sage said.

"Oh, no," Dad told her. "I feel a song coming on."

"Dad, no!" I cried.

But he pushed his chair back and belted out: "It's the hard-knock life for *me*!" Gloria, Sage, and I put our fingers in our ears.

"I'll make them for you anytime you want, if you can get my dad to stop singing," I said.

Across the table, Dad stopped singing and grinned. "It's a deal."

The next day, Dad dropped me off at Mom's earlier than usual. He had a dental convention to attend in Orlando, so he needed to get to the airport. But he'd be back in time for our dinner on Wednesday, which would be "just us," he promised me.

CHAPTER 23

Mom was at the front door waiting when Dad dropped me off. When she asked me how the weekend was, I told her we'd seen Gloria and Sage, and that they'd both loved the cookies. "That's good to hear," Mom said.

"Do you think if you get a boyfriend that he'll have kids?"

"I don't think I'll get to pick and choose the family my new boyfriend comes with," she told me.

"But you wouldn't mind if he had kids, right?"

"I don't mind the idea of dating someone with kids, no," Mom said. "After all, *my* kid is the best thing I've got going for me. But right now I'm not thinking about dating. I'm still settling into life without a husband."

Her voice had taken on a wistful tone. "Just so you know, it's okay with me if you *never* get a boyfriend," I told her.

"Why thank you, Chloe," Mom said, now smiling. "But never is a long time. I think we're getting a little ahead of ourselves here."

"Yeah, I guess. I just meant it's okay with me, no matter what. As long as he's kind."

"You think I'd date someone who wasn't kind?"

"No. Definitely not." She gave me a little hug.

"Speaking of kind. Did you notice the flowers in the window boxes?"

I hadn't, but when I peeked around to look, there they were. Yellow ones. "Is that what you did when I was gone?" I asked.

"It was your friend Lucy," Mom said. "I was out running errands and when I got home she was almost done. She said she wanted it to be a surprise."

"I can't believe she did that," I said. "It's so . . . so kind."

"You're a kind girl," Mom said. "It doesn't surprise me that you have kind friends."

"I should call her to say thank you," I said. Then I paused. "Am I allowed to?"

"Why wouldn't you be?"

"Because I'm grounded."

"I forgot about that. But I think a phone call back to your friend is okay."

"Thanks, Mom," I said. I started to walk away, but I stopped to tell her one more thing. "You know, Lucy's mom died."

"Oh, how awful," Mom said.

"I know. She doesn't ever talk about it. I think it happened a long time ago, and her grandmother lives with her family now. But I was thinking, maybe we can plan a mother/daughter day sometime, and invite her along."

"I think that would be lovely," Mom said.

I went into the kitchen to grab the school directory, along with some lettuce for Captain Carrot, and headed upstairs. Lucy's grandmother answered: "Hello, Tanaka residence."

"Hi, Mrs. Tanaka," I said. "This is Chloe Silver. Lucy's friend."

"Oh, hello, Chloe," she said. "How are you?"

"I'm fine, how are you?"

"Fine, thank you, dear. But I'm guessing you didn't call to chitchat with me, and you want Lucy. She just left to help our neighbor in her backyard."

"You don't mean Mrs. Gallagher, do you?"

"As a matter of fact, I do," she said. "And you're part of that kindness project, too, aren't you?"

I felt a little bit guilty as I said, "Yes."

"I think it's wonderful," Mrs. Tanaka said. "As soon as Lucy gets back, I'll tell her you called."

I'd barely hung up the phone when it rang again, and I pressed to answer. "Hello?"

"Chloe?"

"Yeah?"

"It's Monroe. It's so good you're home. We just called an official meeting of the It Girls."

"I thought meetings were on Tuesday and Thursdays."

"And lunch," Monroe said. "And whenever things come up. Like today, Anjali's aunt just invited her to be a junior bridesmaid in her wedding and we need to look online at dresses."

"That's so cool," I said. "Tell Anjali congratulations."

"You just did," Monroe said. "You're on speaker."

"Oh, hi," I said.

"Hi, Chloe."

"I'm really sorry, but I can't make it today."

"Chloe, now that you're an official It Girl, these meetings are mandatory," Monroe said. "You only get two excused absences a semester. I don't think you should use one now, especially since you have to go to your dad's so often, and you might have to use them for that later. Besides which, this might not even fall under the category of 'excused.' What do you have to do right now that's more important?"

"I'm sort of grounded," I said.

"All right," Monroe said. "Grounded is an excusable absence."

"What are *unexcusable* absences?" I asked.

"Hanging out with other people besides us," Anjali told me.

"We don't have to worry about that with Chloe," Monroe said. "We have an understanding."

"Was that the doorbell?" I heard Anjali ask.

"Rachael must be here," Monroe said.

"I better get off the phone anyway," I said. "My mom probably won't want me on so long."

There was a click, and for a second I thought they'd hung up on me, but then Monroe said, "Okay, I just took you off speaker. Listen, Chloe, you only have one excused absence left. Any more than that, and you're kicked out. Remember that."

"I'll remember," I said.

I hung up and looked over at Cappy. He was munching on his snack, but he paused to look up at me. "I know what you're thinking," I told him. "I'm thinking the same thing." I stood to give him a pat, and then I headed downstairs to make another batch of cookies, with the ingredients left over from Thursday. I told Mom I wanted to bring them to Lucy.

"Hold on," Mom said. "I know I'm not experienced at this grounding thing, but seventy hours of grounding doesn't seem like quite enough for what you put your Dad and me through. Perhaps you can deliver the cookies to Lucy in school tomorrow?"

"I could," I admitted. "But right now I know she's gardening at her neighbor's house. It's part of our project, and I want to go over before she's done."

"All right," Mom said. "As long as you share one of those cookies with me first."

"You got it," I said.

I rang the bell at Lucy's house. Mrs. Tanaka answered, and led me to the backdoor. I spotted Lucy, Mrs. Gallagher, and Theo in the backyard on the other side of the fence. "Hello? Hello?" I called over to them, clutching the package of cookies.

Lucy looked up. "Chloe!" she said. "What are you doing here?"

"I made you cookies to thank you for the flowers," I said. "And I came to help, if you want me to."

"Really?"

"Really," I said. "I mean, we still have the Kindness Club until tomorrow, right?"

Lucy grinned and wiped her brow. "Hey, Mrs. G, is it okay if my friend Chloe comes over?"

I made a move to climb over the fence, but Mrs. Gallagher tsk-tsked. "Come around to the front door and I'll let you in," she told me.

When I got to the backyard, Lucy and Theo took a quick break to each have a cookie, and then we got back to work, pulling weeds. "Mrs. G said you have to be careful not to pull up weeds too fast, or the roots break off and they'll just grow again," Lucy told me.

Mrs. Gallagher had gone back to her seat on the porch, and I turned to look at her, watching us. "When did she call you?" I asked Lucy, my voice lowered.

"She didn't," Lucy replied, just above a whisper. "I called her. Actually, my grandmother did. When we were in school on Friday, she called to see if Mrs. G wanted her to pick the basket up from her front porch. Mrs. G said yes, and she said that she thought my grandmother should keep a better eye on me, and that we should have a talk about the importance of my being kind to my neighbors. Of course my grandma didn't understand that at all, since I *had* been being kind—we all had been!" Lucy's voice raised, and she lowered it again. "The whole time she thought we were playing a prank on her. She couldn't believe we actually meant it when we offered to do nice things. But my grandmother told her about our project, and the club, and she said we could come over after all."

I pulled the weeds, slowly and firmly, and added them to the growing pile at the side of the yard. Lucy said she was planning to plant an herb garden for Mrs. Gallagher, once the place was cleaned up. After a little while, we took a break again. There was fresh lemonade set out, to wash down the cookies.

"Aah, that hits the spot," Lucy said, wiping her upper lip with the back of her palm.

"Did you make this?" Theo asked Mrs. Gallagher.

"Who do you think made it?" she said. "The maid I'm hiding in the kitchen?"

"It's delicious," I said.

"The cookies were, too," Lucy told me.

"Thank you," I said.

"No, thank *you*."

Mrs. Gallagher surveyed the backyard.

"What do you think?" Theo asked her.

"It's starting to look less like a disaster area," she said.

"So you're happy Lucy helped you?"

"Of course I am," she said. "What else would I be?"

"You weren't happy at first," Lucy reminded her.

"It was hard for me to imagine," Mrs. Gallagher said. "Kids in this town don't usually offer any help. They don't so much as offer a wave or a smile."

"Well, Mrs. G," Lucy started. "You don't exactly wave or smile at us. You usually yell instead."

"I know," Mrs. Gallagher said softly. She had a look on her face like she had something more to say, but wasn't sure if she should say it. Finally, she did. "I'll tell you something, though. I wasn't always this way. Sometimes things happen to a person, awful things, and they change you. You see, my husband . . ." Her voice trailed off.

"You have a husband?" Lucy asked.

"I had one," Mrs. Gallagher said. "There was an accident. He was driving on Falls Road. It's a busy road, as you probably know. Not the kind of road you should play ball on, but some kids were—without parents there to watch them, I might add. They were kicking a soccer ball around on the side, and the ball rolled into the street. One of the boys darted out to retrieve it, just as my husband was coming around the curve. He wasn't speeding, but still, he had to swerve to miss hitting the boy, and his car went into a utility pole. It happened just like that."

"He died," Theo said.

Mrs. Gallagher nodded. "My husband, he was the type of person that would rather hurt himself than hurt another person. He didn't want to hurt anything, ever. You would've wanted him in your little kindness club. He'd spend an hour coaxing a fly back out the window before he'd swat it. Once I got so impatient with him, I picked up a shoe to take care of it myself, and he named it. 'May I introduce you to Clement?' he said, because he knew I'd never kill something he'd named—even if that thing was a fly. Thomas was . . ." Mrs. Gallagher paused and took a breath. "He was certainly a better person than I ever was. He was the best person I've ever known, and what happened to him didn't have to happen. Those kids should never have been playing so close to the road. They never should've kicked that ball my husband's way."

"That's why you yelled at Ollie when his soccer ball ended up in your yard," Lucy said.

"I'm sure it was."

"I don't think he knew what happened to your husband," Lucy said. "I didn't."

"Yes, well," Mrs. Gallagher said. "I'm a fairly private person, as you probably know. I don't like to talk about my private life with many people. I certainly shouldn't talk about it with the three of you. You're too young to be bothered with the sadness of an old woman."

"I'm glad you did tell us," Lucy said. "I wish we'd talked before. I would've . . . I would've been kinder all along, if I'd known."

I remembered the quote I'd found on the day we'd started the Kindness Club: "Be kind, for everyone you meet is fighting a hard battle." I understood what Plato, whoever he was, meant now. He meant that life is hard for everyone, even in ways you can't see. Life was hard for Mrs. Gallagher, because she missed her husband. Life was hard for Sage, because she missed her dad. Life was hard for Monroe, too. And it was important to be kind.

"I'm glad we got to help you today," I told Mrs. Gallagher. "And I'm sorry about your husband."

"Me too," Theo said.

Lucy smiled a sad smile. "Me three."

"Thank you," Mrs. Gallagher said. "You know, the three of you taught me something I didn't know before today. At my age, it's not often you learn something new, but I did. I didn't think I'd ever find a reason to be happy again, after Thomas died. But today, watching you in the yard, I did. You kids . . . you don't know how this feels."

"We do," Theo said. "And we know why, too. It's the serotonin in your brain."

"Well, I don't know about that," she said. "But you did more than change my backyard today. You changed my life." Then she frowned. "A shame fall is coming and the leaves will mess up the yard again."

"But the colors will be so pretty," I said.

"Do you always try to find the bright side of things?" Mrs. Gallagher asked.

"Yes," I said. "As a matter of fact, I do."

"My husband was like that. He used to tell me to look for the silver linings."

"I found one!" Lucy said. "A *Chloe* Silver lining!"

By then it was starting to get late—not dark yet, but if we waited too much longer, it would be. We put the pulled-up weeds in a garbage bag and brought it out to the curb. Mrs. Gallagher thanked us again. Theo and I walked Lucy to her door. "So we're all set for tomorrow, right?" Theo said. "I'll bring the report, and then the three of us can talk about what happened with Mrs. Gallagher."

"Yup," Lucy said.

"We can go over it more at lunch," I said.

"You won't be sitting with the It Girls?" Lucy asked.

I shook my head. "Did you plant the flowers at my house because you wanted to get my serotonin level up?"

"Did it work?" Lucy asked.

"Yes," I told her. "Being your friend makes me happy, and I can't sit with the It Girls at lunch tomorrow, because I'll be with my other club."

CHAPTER 24

The next day, lunch went exactly as you would expect. After I got my sandwich, instead of going to the It Girls table, I headed over to the members of the Kindness Club. Lucy was wearing two of Oliver's ties around her neck, one yellow and one green, like yellow and green pencil cases, or like yellow flowers and their green stems. Theo was talking about a storm that was gathering strength in the Atlantic Ocean. "It's Tropical Storm Doris right now," he said. "But it may turn into *Hurricane* Doris soon."

Lucy speared a cubed piece of cheese with her fork, but paused before popping it into her mouth. "Why do they name storms anyway?"

"It's easier to track them that way," Theo said. "Before the nineteen-fifties, they just referred to storms by year and the order they occurred."

"Hmm," Lucy said. "I guess it's a bit easier to remember where you were for Hurricane Stanley, than where you were for the second storm of two thousand and twelve."

"It's massively easier," Theo said. "Storms can occur at the same time, for one thing. And for another, humans process memories—"

"Chloe," a voice behind us said gravely. Monroe's voice.

Theo didn't finish his thought. I turned around. "Hi, Monroe," I said. "Theo was just telling us a true story about tropical storms."

Lucy and Theo both smiled, but Monroe did not. "I like your necklace," Lucy told her.

"What's that supposed to mean?"

"That I like it," Lucy said.

Monroe slipped it into her shirt so you couldn't see it anymore. "Is this some sort of last-minute science project meeting?" she asked me.

"Sort of," I said. "But mostly because I wanted to have lunch with them."

"Chloe, we discussed this."

"I know, but—"

"But nothing," she told me. "You know, I wasn't supposed to invite anyone into the club unless all members approved the invitation first. It's a rule. *I* wrote that rule."

"I know."

"I made an exception for you."

"I really appreciate it," I told her. "I want to be in your club, *and* I want to be in this one. You could be in the Kindness Club, too. I mean, it's also up to my fellow club members, but if you want—"

"You must be kidding me," Monroe said. "I don't want to be in the stupid club you have with them. And it's not possible for you to be in both, either. You have to pick. Their club, or my club."

I felt everyone's eyes on me. "Well then," I said, "I'm sorry, but if I can't be in both, I pick the Kindness Club."

"So you lied again. You told me you wanted to be an It Girl. Well, don't think for a second that you're rejecting me right now, because I'm rejecting you. I'm taking back your invitation. And what's more—"

Her voice caught, and for a moment I thought she might cry.

But she just narrowed her eyes, and went on. "What's more is this. I went out on a limb for you—twice. But there won't be a third chance. I won't ever make the mistake of being your friend again. But you guys—" Her eyes shifted between Lucy, Theo, and me. "You guys deserve each other."

And with that, she turned on her heels and left us.

"Whoa," Lucy said softly. I didn't speak. I just followed Monroe with my eyes, as she walked back to her table. There was a part of me that felt a little bit *unkind*, for wanting her to make the exception, and then letting her down. After all, Monroe was fighting battles, too.

But then I turned back to Lucy and Theo, and I realized that I belonged with them. Even if Lucy had a style unlike anyone else's. And even if Theo had no style, and was a bit obsessed with his work. They were still the kindest people I'd met since moving to Braywood, and when it came to having things in common, kindness was what mattered most. I'd never choose to be in a club they weren't allowed to be part of.

That afternoon, when we walked into the science lab, Mr. Dibble was not standing in the front of the room. Instead there was an exceptionally tall woman in a lab coat. A name was written on the board behind her: *Dr. Eleanor Whelan*. The name sounded familiar, but I couldn't place it.

We all filed in, and she cleared her throat to quiet us all down, and rapped the board with a long ruler. "I am Dr. Eleanor Whelan," she said. "I'll be taking over this class, and Mr. Dibble will return exclusively to his duties as principal. I went to Harvard and Yale, where I earned degrees in both biology and chemistry, and I helped author that book you all have on your desks. So now you know a bit about me. Please open your textbooks to page thirty-six."

There were the sounds of kids swiping through pages to get to the right one. Down the table, Theo had his hand raised. "Excuse me, Dr. Whelan?" he said.

"Yes?"

"Mr. Dibble had assigned special projects to us."

There was a chorus of groans, and someone said, "Don't tell her."

But Theo went on: "Each table of students was its own group," he said. "And every week, a different group had to give a report."

"I see," Dr. Whelan said. "Well, that's not on my syllabus. So you won't have to worry about that this semester."

There were whoops from the other kids.

"Now to page thirty-six—"

"But Lucy, Chloe, and I already did our report!" Theo said.

"Teacher's pets," a voice called. Monroe's voice.

"That's enough," Dr. Whelan said. I honestly didn't know if she was speaking to Theo, or speaking to Monroe. But it didn't matter. The three of us looked at each other sadly. And then we opened up our textbooks to page thirty-six, because we didn't have any other choice.

At the end of the day, Theo suggested we take things up with Mr. Dibble himself. After all, Theo maintained, it wasn't fair for us to be in the exact same position as the other kids in class, when the three of us were the only ones who'd had to do extra work. At the very least, Dr. Whelan should excuse us from a quiz, or give us bonus points.

So we headed to the principal's office. The receptionist pressed a button on her phone to call to Mr. Dibble. He must've told her to send us in, because that's what she did.

Mr. Dibble stood up and gave us each a fist bump. There were piles of paper all over his desk, on the windowsill, and on every chair except for the one Mr. Dibble had been sitting in. "Sorry I can't offer you seats," he said. "I've been buried these past couple weeks, performing double duty as a principal and science teacher. It's a good thing I just gave up one of those jobs."

"That's actually what we wanted to talk to you about," Theo said. "You picked us as the first group to give a report."

"Ah, yes, I remember," Mr. Dibble said, in a voice that made me wonder if he really did. "Well, you're off the hook now."

"But we finished it!" Theo said. "It was due today! We told Dr. Whelan about it, and she didn't seem to care."

Mr. Dibble sank back down into his seat. "I'm sorry, kids," he said. "Dr. Whelan insisted on using her own syllabus as a condition for coming here, and we had to say yes. She's an excellent teacher—one of the very best in the business."

"She wrote our textbook," Lucy said.

"Yes," Mr. Dibble said. "We were lucky to get her—especially at this late date. But I will try to think of a way to make it up to you."

A breeze came through the open window, sending a bunch of the piles on Mr. Dibble's desk down to the floor. We bent to help him pick them up. He thanked us, and we started to walk out, but he called us back. "Wait, you three. Don't I at least get to know what the project was?"

Theo pulled our report out of his backpack. It was all typed up, with a very professional-looking cover. "You said we could be creative," Theo reminded him, as Mr. Dibble began to flip through the pages.

"That's right," Mr. Dibble said. "I give points for creativity. What made you think of this?"

"Well, Chloe always does kind things," Lucy said. "And we wondered what effect that would have on people who aren't. That was the beginning of it."

"Very interesting," Mr. Dibble said.

"It didn't work on everyone," I admitted. "There was one girl . . . well, I used to think being kind was easy. I actually didn't think about it that much. And sometimes that's what it's like. The kind thing is there, right in front of you, and you do it. But sometimes it's hard to figure out. Sometimes you have to be kind when you don't want to be, and sometimes people don't even want your kindness. Sometimes it doesn't change them at all."

"That may be true," Mr. Dibble said. "But keep in mind, just because you didn't see the effects of your kindness in the case of that girl, doesn't mean it didn't change her. Maybe you encouraged her to be kind to someone else down the line, and on and on. Before you know it, you have changed the lives of people you'll never even know. I remember learning about the butterfly effect when I was just about your age."

"Theo told us about it," Lucy said. "If a butterfly flaps its wings, it can cause a hurricane on the other side of the world."

"Exactly," Mr. Dibble said. "It's not always a storm that's set into motion when we act. Think of the things you set into motion with this project—the positive side of the butterfly effect. The neighbor in your report—what do you think she will do now that you've been kind to her?"

Lucy shrugged. "I don't know," she said.

"We can't know," Theo said. "That's the part of the butterfly effect that's impossible to measure."

"True," Mr. Dibble said. "But I suspect 'Mrs. G,' as you call her here, will find opportunities for kindness where she wouldn't have in the past, and perhaps the people she is kind to will do the same. It reminds me of Newton's third law of motion."

"There's another one?" Lucy asked. "Wow, Newton was a busy guy."

"Every action has an equal and opposite reaction," Theo supplied.

"And in this case, you put the actions in motion," Mr. Dibble said. "I knew you kids would come up with the right questions to ask. And I knew you'd make important discoveries, the ripples of which could go global."

"Did you hear that, Theo?" Lucy asked.

"I did," he said.

"You know," Mr. Dibble went on, "part of the reason I wanted to open the classroom up to this kind of project was because of the lessons I remember from being your age. Not just the ones I learned from my teachers, but the ones I learned from the kids, too. Trust me, when you're my age, you will remember this. May I keep your report?"

"Of course," Theo told him.

He put it on his desk. "This is one for the pile that I'm happy to have. Excellent work, you three."

We said good-bye and headed out. "I have my doubts about him remembering to make it up to us," Theo said, once we were back in the hall.

"You want to hear something funny," I said, and Theo nodded for me to continue. "I don't really mind. I'm glad we did the project. Even if we don't get credit."

"Me too," Lucy said.

"Yeah, well," Theo said. "It's not like it affected my GPA in a negative way, so I guess I don't, either."

"I think we should keep the club," I said. "There's no rule that it has to end just because the project is over. We can keep being kind."

"Do you mean I should keep doing dishes for Anabelle every night?"

"No," I said. "I don't think being kind means your sister *always* gets to have her way. She can do the dishes sometimes."

"Unlike Mrs. G, who can't tend her garden because of her back," Lucy said.

"And unlike Monroe, who doesn't want me to do any more kindnesses for her," I added. "She'd probably consider it unkind if I did. But I can help you in Mrs. Gallagher's yard. I'll clean up her leaves when they fall."

"I will, too," Theo said.

"And maybe," I went on, "we can help other people who can't garden for themselves. Or if their cars are really dirty and we could wash them for free. Or we could leave quarters by vending machines . . . or . . . or . . ."

"Or a million things!" Lucy said.

"We should make a list," Theo said. "And we should categorize the different kinds of kindnesses. Some take up a lot more time than others. And some take more people."

"I declare a meeting after school to discuss all the possibilities!" Lucy said. "What do you say?"

"Well, I'm sort of grounded," I told her. "I better go home right now. But can we have a makeup meeting? Like at lunch tomorrow?"

"Absolutely," she said.

"See you at our table," Theo said.

CHAPTER 25

I ran all the way home and called Mom before I'd even taken off my backpack. She wasn't at her desk, but I left a message. Then I pressed the button to hang up the phone, and I planned to get a snack, and go upstairs to see Captain Carrot and get started on my homework. But before I did all that, I had one more call to make, and I dialed a phone number I'd known by heart since the first grade.

"Hey, Chloe!" Lia said. "How's the It Girls Club?"

"Oh, well, actually that's why I was calling," I told her. "Because the thing is, I'm not in that club anymore. I'm in a different club. We started it for a science project. We wanted to see if we could change people's brains by being nice to them."

"You wanted to change people's *brains*?" she asked.

"We changed the chemicals in their brains," I said. "We didn't have an MRI machine, so we couldn't check for sure. But we tried some things out on a few people that weren't so kind, and then they acted kind back."

"That's cool."

"I know. And we decided to keep the club and keep doing kind things. We have a meeting tomorrow to discuss our next kindness projects."

"Is this you and Monroe?"

"No, Monroe isn't in this one. It's me and two other kids, Lucy and Theo. And they're not exactly popular. At first I didn't think they were the right friends for me, and I was upset that I had to work with them. But I was totally wrong about them."

"What's your new club called?" Lia asked.

"The Kindness Club," I told her.

"That sounds cool."

"Do you really think so?"

"Of course," she said. "It's perfect for you too. You've always been the kindest person I know. Last week I was walking home with Trissa, and I dropped a few pennies along the way. I told her how you taught me to do that, so other people could find lucky pennies."

"You talk about me?"

"Of course I do."

"Did Trissa think it was dumb?"

"No! She dropped her pennies, too. And listen to this— she told me you should make sure to put them on the ground head-side up, because that makes lucky pennies even luckier."

"Oh, wow," I said. "I never knew that. But I'll bring that up at the next Kindness Club meeting."

The caller ID beeped in, and when I checked the screen I saw it was Mom's office number. "Listen, that's my mom," I told Lia. "So I have to go. But when you come visit me, I'll make you an honorary member of the Kindness Club, if you want."

"I'd love it!" she said.

We said good-bye, and I clicked over and said, "Hi, Mom. I'm safe and sound."

"Oh, good. How's everything at home?"

"Fine. How's everything at the office?"

"It's getting better," she said. "It was a pretty good day."

"That's great," I told her.

"Yes, it is," she said. "How about you? Did you have fun with your friends in school?"

A familiar line ran through my head:

I have the best friends in my new school.

Right then I realized why yellow flowers meant friend- ship, because having friends made you feel light inside. "You know what, Mom," I said. "I totally did."

★ ACKNOWLEDGMENTS ★

Gratitude is another thing that increases a person's happiness, and when it comes to this book, I am happily grateful to so many people:

First of all, to Libba Bray, whose supreme kindness on a supremely cold day got me thinking about other kindness stories.

To Sarah Mlynowski, Jennifer E. Smith, and Robin Wasserman, who brainstormed with me until we came up with the perfect concept—and the perfect series title.

To my wonderful readers (and re-readers): Lindsay Aaronson, Michael Buckley, Jen Calonita, Lia Carson, Gitty Daneshvari, Julia DeVillers, Rachel Feld, Jackie Friedland, Adele Griffin, Katie Hartman, Melissa Losquadro, Wendy Mass, Jess Rothenberg, Leila Sales, Laura Schechter, Bianca Turetsky, Kai Williams, and Meg Wolitzer.

To all my friends who have shown me incredible kind-ness, again and again and again. Shout-outs to my weekly (sometimes daily) sounding boards: Amy Bressler, Erin Cummings, Jennifer Daly, Regan Hofmann, Arielle Warshall Katz, Logan Levkoff, Geralyn Lucas, and Katie Stein.

To my elementary school/middle school test-readers: Abigail, Anjali, Asher, Chase, Daniel, Lia, Livy, Maverick, Rachael, Sasha, Sara, and Tesa. And special thanks to Avery Aaronson and Chloe Brawer, for their amazing notes; and to Madden and Brody Shuffler, who skipped watching a foot-ball game to listen to me read the first draft of this book, from beginning to end. (If that's not kindness, I don't know what is.)

To Laura Dail and Tamar Rydzinski, at the Laura Dail Literary Agency, Inc., for taking such good care of the things I write (and of me).

To my editor, Mary Kate Castellani, who stuck with me through every version of Chloe's story, until we got to the right one; to the Bloomsbury team: Eshani Agrawal, Colleen Andrews, Diane Aronson, Erica Barmash, Beth Eller, Courtney Griffin, Melissa Kavonic, Linette Kim, Cindy Loh, Donna Mark, Lizzy Mason, Catherine Onder, Emily Ritter, and Claire Stetzer; to Nancy Seitz, for her careful read of the manuscript; and to Kim Smith, for the cutest cover ever.

Finally, always, to my father, Joel Sheinmel; to my

mother, Elaine Sheinmel, and my stepdad, Phil Getter; to my sister, Alyssa Sheinmel, and my brother-in-law, JP Gravitt; to my stepsiblings, their spouses, and all of their children; and to our entire extended, wacky, wonderful family: thank you for being kind and for being mine.

Love,

Courtney